THE TROUBLE WITH TABBIES

A Love & Pets Romantic Comedy, Book 2

A.G. HENLEY

CENTRAL PARK BOOKS

Summary: A cat-loving young woman hires a fake fiancé to help her get an inheritance to fund a feline rescue and adoption center.

CONTENTS

Hey, readers!   vii

Chapter 1   1
Chapter 2   6
Chapter 3   13
Chapter 4   19
Chapter 5   24
Chapter 6   27
Chapter 7   30
Chapter 8   32
Chapter 9   36
Chapter 10   40
Chapter 11   43
Chapter 12   48
Chapter 13   51
Chapter 14   57
Chapter 15   60
Chapter 16   65
Chapter 17   72
Chapter 18   80
Chapter 19   85
Chapter 20   92
Chapter 21   99
Chapter 22   103
Chapter 23   108
Chapter 24   110
Chapter 25   115
Chapter 26   121
Chapter 27   127
Chapter 28   134
Chapter 29   139
Chapter 30   142

Chapter 31   147
Chapter 32   151
Chapter 33   155
Chapter 34   161
Chapter 35   167
Chapter 36   170
Chapter 37   174
Chapter 38   177
Epilogue   180

Read Next   185
Acknowledgments   191
Also by A.G. Henley   193
About the Author   195

Hey, readers!

Get the FREE prequel ebook to the Love & Pets series, *Love, Pugs, and Other Problems,* an exclusive short story that tells how Amelia gets Doug the pug instead of a ring! Go to aghenley.com/free-books

Chapter One

Beatrix

I swing my Range Rover into one of the last available parking spaces outside the Thirsty Lion Brewery and turn off the engine. A soft meow comes from the back seat.

I turn and smile into the bright green eyes of Fluffernutter, my tiny tuxedo cat who's peering out of the soft-sided carrier I'd strapped in with the seat belt.

"Ready?" I ask.

Fluff meows again, which I interpret as a yes. I get out, unbuckle the carrier, take the last in a long series of deep, settling breaths, and enter the fray.

Most days, the Thirsty Lion is a low-key craft brewery in Evergreen, a small town in the foothills west of Denver, Colorado. People come here to hike, bike, fish, or to enjoy a pint and the scenery on a sweet, summery afternoon.

But one Saturday in July every year, the Thirsty Lion hosts Colorado Cat Rescue's big annual event: Colorado Adopts Cats, a fund raiser and cat adoption event. Today's that day. People sit at tables with beers, listening to music, while others cruise the shade tents nearby that offer everything from cat toys to locally produced cat food.

I beeline toward CCR's large tent set up in the center of the event, scratching one arm and then the other as I walk. I feel my face redden, and I haven't even had to speak to anyone yet. Some people are allergic to cats. Not me. People give me hives.

I enter the tent, and the sight of all those cats in cages focuses me. Big and small, short and long haired, monochrome or with distinctive markings, the cats and kittens prowl, prance, and tumble around the enclosures like living fur balls. They're every imaginable combination of breeds, from the common American shorthair to a rare Manx with its unusually short tail.

I lift Fluff up in her carrier so she can see and hear all the cats better. She stares unblinking at the mass of felines, her tail twitching like she's found a bird, squirrel, and mouse hot-tubbing together in her water bowl.

People walk among the cages, pointing and smiling at various cats. Families, couples, singles—they're all here to adopt rescue cats. I push my glasses up my nose and swipe the tear of happiness that leaks out of one eye.

"Beatrix! You made it!" Vilma, a middle-aged Latina with a bright green event t-shirt, ankle-length patterned maxi skirt, and closed-toed hiking sandals waves me over to a table at the center of the tent. It's covered in pamphlets about CCR, stuffed cats for purchase to support the nonprofit, and sample bags of cat food.

"Ooh, I love your shirt!" she says.

I glance down to remind myself what I'm wearing; it's my *I didn't choose the cat lady life, the cat lady life chose me* tee today.

"And *hola* to you, too, *dulzura*." Vilma, CCR's executive director, coos at Fluff through the carrier gate. She'd met Fluff several times when I'd brought her to board meetings. She probably thinks I'm a kook for toting an emotional support cat everywhere I go, but she's always welcomed us.

"Looks like you have a good turnout," I say.

She puffs out a breath and pushes her wiry gray-brown hair out of her face. "It's been a lot of work to pull together, like every year. But Bea," she clutches my hand in hers, "we could not have done this without your financial support. I wish you would let me acknowledge you in our materials or on the website."

I cradle Fluff and her carrier under my free arm and look around at the milling people smiling and laughing at the antics of all the cats. "It's enough to know that so many of these fur babies will have homes after today. And that we'll get the permanent adoption center built soon."

Vilma hands a brochure to a man browsing the table beside me. "Thank you for supporting the homeless cats of Colorado." When he moves away, she turns back to me. "After we recover from this weekend, we'll set up a board meeting for planning. Maybe in early September?"

"Perfect," I say, but unease shoots through me. I'd promised Vilma I'd help pay for the center. The problem is, I don't have the money yet.

I love cats—a lot. I've rescued dozens myself, and I support CCR as much as I can with my own income writing romance books, but this is an expensive project. I need my portion of the money from our family trust, my inheritance, which my father has promised to give me . . . soon.

A harried-looking man with thinning white hair and wearing the same green shirt as Vilma rushes over to us.

"Vilma, sweetpea, I think one of the kittens needs medical help. She's thrown up a few times and is looking peaky. Oh, hello, Bea, so good to see you." Robert, Vilma's husband and another member of the CCR board, shakes my free hand. His smile is yellow, crooked, and radiant. "We're getting incredible interest in the event; Channel 9 is stopping by to film soon for the five o'clock news."

"That's wonderful," I say. "You're doing great work."

"And you, Bea. You are, too." Vilma beams at me, then turns

to Robert, all business. "Dr. Travis is outside. Take the sick *gatita* to him. He said he'd squeeze in any of our cats that need to be seen between his scheduled patients."

"Dr. Travis is here?" I ask.

Vilma smiles. "You know him?" She presses her hands to her chest. "Such a kind man."

"He's my veterinarian . . . I mean my cats' veterinarian." *Duh, Bea.* "I can take the sick kitten out to him."

Vilma looks grateful, and distracted, as another green-shirted volunteer calls to her from a nearby cage where a family seems to have chosen a sweet ragdoll to adopt. "*Gracias*, Beatrix, that would be so helpful."

Robert leads me to a cage sitting by itself along the side of the tent. "She's over here in the makeshift infirmary. I'll be back in a snap with a cat carrier."

A tiny gray Russian blue cat hunches in a corner of the cage. I can tell at a glance that the kitten isn't well. Her ears are down, and she's panting. Poor thing.

"What do you think is wrong with her, Fluff?" I ask my cat in a low voice. I don't actually expect her to respond. I'm not *that* much of a cat lady. Good thing, too, because she doesn't.

The sickly kitten doesn't even look our way. My heart double thumps. I can't stand to see any animal suffer. Robert returns, reaches into the cage, gently scoops up the kitten, and places her in the carrier. She doesn't resist.

He hands her over and flashes his toothy grin before he walks away. "Thank you again, Beatrix. I'm back to the trenches."

I tell him goodbye and, a carrier in each hand, hurry outside to find Travis Brewer, DVM. How did I miss him on the way in? I must be more anxious than I thought. I squint, searching the grounds.

There it is. The bright blue-green recreational vehicle with the Love & Pets Mobile Animal Clinic logo painted on the side is parked in a corner of the Thirsty Lion's lot. As I approach, I spot a sign on the door asking people to wait. The staff is with a patient.

I settle on a nearby bench, cat carriers on both sides, and pull out my phone to pass the time. I check my social media pages quickly, responding apologetically to a few disappointed comments about the delay of the release of my next book. Trust me, no one's more disappointed in the delay than me. Then, I open Gmail. Hearing from readers makes my day. Who am I kidding? It makes my month.

Instead, an email from my older sister, Aggie, waits unopened at the top of my email pile. With a familiar panicky jolt in my stomach, I click on it.

Beatrix, she begins. She never calls me by my nickname, Bea. And she hates that I still use her childhood nickname, Aggie. "It's *Agatha*, Beatrix," she says every time.

I'm hosting an 80th birthday party for Father. Family only. He wants you to come and to bring your boyfriend. And he wants to discuss your inheritance.

Although I knew this day would come, my hands shake and my heart pounds.

Aggie gave the date of the party, three weeks away, at the end of the email. I shove the phone back in my pocket, the cheerful sounds of the event suddenly muffled.

Not going home to Aspen isn't an option. I can tell from Aggie's tone that Dad ordered me to be there. In our family, that's like an emailed summons from God. Which means very soon Dad, my three older siblings—Aggie, Thomas, and Henry —and their spouses will inspect and judge me, and I'll be found wanting. Well, not Henry so much, but the others for sure.

And the panic-inducing prospect of spending time with my family is only part of the trouble. The real problem is that I have to bring my boyfriend.

A boyfriend . . . that doesn't exist.

Chapter Two

Beatrix

The RV door opens, and Dr. Travis steps out. He's wearing short-sleeved navy scrubs, and his shoulder-length black hair is in a loose ponytail. A pretty blonde woman in pink scrubs with bug-eyed cartoon pugs all over them follows him. I recognize her. Travis brought her to my house a while ago to help with vaccination day.

I only approach after their patient, a bearded man holding a cat carrier of his own, walks away. Travis grins and waves at me. He looks genuinely pleased to see me, but I look away, uncomfortable as always.

Travis puts a hand on the blonde woman's back. "Amelia, do you remember Beatrix Fuller?"

"Yes, of course! I'll never forget it. That was my first day as your unofficial vet tech."

Amelia greets me, and I nod and smile. I'll bet that day was memorable for more than one reason. She bravely held on to each of my dozens of spitting, biting, scratching cats while Travis vaccinated them. That day's a disaster of feline proportions every year.

She peeks into the carriers I'm holding. "Who do you have there?" Travis peers in, too.

I hold up the kitten. "One of Vilma's rescues is sick." I lift Fluff. "This is my cat. She's along for the ride."

It's always awkward explaining why I have a cat everywhere I go. The nice thing about pet people is that if they think it's strange to bring a cat to an event where you're supposed to take cats home, they don't show it.

Travis takes the kitten's carrier from me. "Amelia will help with the exam, if that's okay. She's in school to be a veterinary technician now. She's trying to get practical experience on weekends when she can."

Something about his proud smile as he leads the way inside the RV tells me they're more than friends or colleagues now. Good. Travis has always seemed a little lonely. It takes one to know one.

Inside the RV, cabinets run the length of one side with stainless steel countertops and a sink. An exam table is folded up against the wall, and several stacked cages are secured against the side of the vehicle for holding patients. The windows are half open, letting in a breeze.

"When did I see you last, Bea?" Travis asks as he washes his hands. "It's been a few months, hasn't it?"

I think about it. "You came to see Scruffy and Malcolm when they were sick."

He nods. "Upper respiratory infections. I remember."

"How is school going?" I ask Amelia.

Her eyes go wide with excitement as she lowers the exam table and cleans it with a spray bottle and towel. "It's so much fun! I never even thought about working with animals before I met Travis. I worked in an incredibly boring law office before. I had no idea how much I needed a different job—one where I can do some good. When I took those career tests in high school, they always told me I should be a vending machine servicer or a fiberglass laminator or something. I think I filled in the wrong circles." She flutters a hand. "Anyway, I've been learning to draw blood, check for parasites, assist with surgeries, and work with, er, difficult patients." She glances at me.

"Like my cats?" I raise an amused eyebrow.

"No! I mean . . . yes . . . I mean, yours are only hard because there are so many of them. But you're so generous to give them all homes," she hurries to add.

"Bea is the patron saint of rescue cats. Saint Beatrix." Travis says. "We should get you a badge or crown or something." We laugh, and Amelia looks relieved that she didn't offend me. He nods at her, obvious affection on his face. "Amelia's also been overhauling my office processes, like scheduling and invoicing, and generally being a huge help."

Her face grows pink to match her scrubs. "And the one-year anniversary of our first date is in a few weeks."

"Congratulations." Watching them, my heart lurches painfully. Visions of a forgotten black and blue shaving razor in my medicine cabinet and a man's hiking jacket in my hall closet bubble in my brain. I rub my temple to massage them away. I have the relationship memories of a bitter old lady.

Travis sets the kitten's carrier on the table. "So what's wrong with this girl?"

I pass on what Robert told Vilma and me while Travis gently examines the cat. The kitten doesn't struggle; her green eyes are dull. Not good signs.

"Could be gastritis . . . something she ate," he says, "but I should get some blood work."

Amelia opens a drawer and collects a vial and other supplies, and Travis puts on latex gloves. He takes the kitten's blood while Amelia holds her. When the blood draw is finished, Amelia sets the kitten gently back in her carrier.

"Hey, speaking of anniversaries, the second annual Love & Pets Party is in a month. Will you come?" Amelia gestures to a flyer tacked on a bulletin board secured to the inside door of the RV.

A cloud passes over Travis's face as he glances at the flyer, too. I understand why. He and Jo, his grandmother, organized the first party last year as a community event for pets and their owners. Along with bringing in music, food trucks, and all kinds of pet vendors, Travis offered free and low cost vaccinations and exams for pets whose owners couldn't usually afford them. It was a fantastic event, like this one. But right before the party, Jo passed away. I'm sure it's a poignant reminder of her.

"Of course." I try to support pet adoption events whenever I can, and I especially want to help Travis out. Not many vets would come to someone's home and face the number of cats I have. I went last year but had to leave early when a panic attack hit. Pretty much the story of my life the last few years.

"Great! You can meet Doug and Daisy, our pugs," Amelia says. "We bring them on calls sometimes, but they don't fit together in one cage and they whine when they're apart, so we have to leave them at home most of the time. Not that they mind. They're in *love*." She pulls a face.

I hadn't heard all the details, but I knew the pugs were involved in bringing Amelia and Travis together. If even pugs can find love, what's wrong with me? Like I said, bitter old lady.

Travis takes off his gloves. "I'll let Vilma know what I think we should do for the kitten as soon as I can."

"You can call me. I'll foster the kitten until she's better, and I'll pay for today, too." I knew I would foster her the second I saw her. And I'll have help: one of my cats, BooBoo, likes mothering the foster kittens.

"That's kind of you, Bea. Your cats are due for vaccinations, too. Do you want to schedule something now?"

"I wish I could, but I have to go home the next few weeks and see my family."

Amelia nods politely, but Travis raises an eyebrow at me. I'd told him a little about my family during appointments. I don't have many people to talk to, and he's always a good listener. He waits, probably seeing I have more to say.

I hesitate, not wanting to take up their time, but Aggie's email and its implications swirl sickeningly around my head.

"Everything okay?" he asks.

I run a hand through my straight brown hair. "No, not really. I . . . have a problem."

"We've got a few minutes." He unfolds two stools that were secured against the wall, and Amelia and I sit.

She watches me with concern, making me wonder how bad I must look. Acutely aware of how my rich-kid problem must sound when I say it out loud, I explain the situation haltingly.

"The thing is," I finish, "I got so tired of hearing about how I should find a successful guy to settle down with at every holiday and get-together, I *might* have told my family about my fabulous boyfriend. A guy I've been dating for two years now and love with all my heart. Who conveniently can never go home with me and is out of town whenever one of my siblings stops in to see me."

"Wow," Travis says. "So you need to present this made up boyfriend to your family? What happens if you don't? What if you just tell them the truth?"

I pull Fluff's carrier onto my lap, reach inside, and run my hand over her patterned black and white fur, willing my breathing to slow.

"My family's very . . . traditional. Especially when it comes to money, but a lot of other things, too. My father believes his children should be settled before they receive their inheritance. And by that, he means—"

"Married." Amelia finishes my sentence.

I roll my eyes and nod. "If we aren't married, we're supposed to get the inheritance when we turn twenty-eight, but my birthday was last month. I'm guessing my father is having second thoughts." About his disappointing youngest daughter. I push the hurt away. "I have a career and I can support myself without a man or my family's money." They don't need to hear all the gory details about my fading book sales. "But I was counting on the inheritance to help Vilma pay for CCR's no-kill cat rescue facility. She already has the plans and a general contractor lined up. They just need funding."

Vilma has a lot of innovative ideas about animal care and adoption. She wants to expand to dogs, other domestic pets, and even wildlife in the next few years. But for now, she'll take in every cat that needs a home.

"Without the money I promised, they don't have enough." I swallow hard. "And without my inheritance, *I* don't have enough." I shouldn't have told Vilma I'd help before I had the money in hand, but I want this so badly.

Travis pats my shoulder. "You're a good egg, Bea. I wish more people cared about cats as much as you do. Maybe you should tell Vilma you have to delay for a while. Talk to your father about your plans for the money. I'll bet he'll be so proud of you, he'll sign it right over."

"That won't work." My obsession with cats is one of the many things my father doesn't understand about me at best and dislikes about me at worst. He isn't likely to agree that a cat adoption center is a good use of the money.

"Maybe there's another way . . ." Amelia chews on her lip. "I saw a movie once where a woman needed to be in a serious relationship to convince her boss that she was ready for a promotion. So she hired a guy she met at a wedding to be her fiancé. They were supposed to split once she was promoted, but instead they fell in love. It was so sweet."

I nod. The fake relationship—a tried and true romance trope. Authors used it in book plots all the time to bring otherwise unlikely couples together.

Amelia claps her hands. "This could totally work! You put an ad on a dating app or Craigslist or somewhere, do phone interviews to rule out the creepers, and then you two get to know each other quickly before taking him to meet your father."

Travis chuckles. "Are you seriously advising Bea to do this, Amelia? I'm glad we treat pets and not humans."

"Thanks for the idea, but I couldn't pull something like that off." Even the thought of trying it sends something slithery and slimy through my stomach. Lying successfully to my family aside, I'd probably hire a mass murderer, or worse, a cat hater.

"Well, it worked out in that movie." Amelia looks disappointed.

Travis glances out the window. "I hate to break up the brainstorming session, but our next patient is waiting."

I collect my two carriers. "Thank you for listening."

"Of course! Any time." Amelia hugs me, and I manage not to shrink away. "Think about my idea."

Travis opens the door to the RV and helps me outside, where two women wait with a Maine coon the size of a small lab.

My thoughts heavy, I head back to the adoption tent to update Vilma about the kitten. Looking around at the families perusing the cages of cats, picking out their new fur children, I know I have to find a way to ensure CCR gets its facility.

Somehow.

But there's no way I'll hire a guy to pretend to love me and want to marry me. I might write romance, but I live in the real world. Here, love and marriage is something that happens to other people. Not to me.

Chapter Three

Beatrix

The sun melts into the cloud-covered horizon, and Belle's heart sinks with it. He's not coming, at least not today. She turns toward the dark, empty cabin, unsure how many dark, lonely nights she can endure.

At the last moment the clouds break, allowing a pink hue to spiral across the sky . . . and she sees him. Nathaniel. He rides toward her, his horses' hooves moving slower than the three years he spent away from her fighting this cursed war.

Her eyes lock on him as he advances across the prairie. After what seems an eternity upon an eternity, he reaches her and dismounts. She can't move, can't speak; her body shivers with anticipation.

Her reaches for her and encircles her waist with his strong hands. His steady gaze seems to study her very soul.

"Belle," Nathaniel says, "I —"

I pause, my hands poised over the keyboard. What does Nathaniel say? What does a man say to the woman he loves but hasn't seen in years? I crack my knuckles, waiting for the words to come to me.

A screeching tangle of fur and claws explode into my home office. Two of my cats, Raspberry and Kit Kat, tear across the carpet, up onto the small file cabinet beside the desk and roll across my keyboard, sending the screen into chaos. I scramble out of their way.

Fluff, who *was* contentedly purring in my lap, springs straight up and darts out of the office, scratching my thighs through my pajama pants in the process. I do my best to separate the fighters, but it's like jumping into the middle of a wrestling match where the competitors have claws and fangs instead of hands. I'm more likely to get shredded than they are to stop going at each other. They charge out of the office, too, before I can get to them.

"Ow." The scratches sting. I pull my pants down a little to peer at my leg. Yep, I'm bleeding. Yet another feline-related injury. But I sit back down. I have to finish this all-important scene, and it's not the first time I'll write bloodied.

The office is warm and still as I wait, fingers on the keyboard again, for the words to appear in my head and make their way to the screen. My fingers crawl—not fly, they haven't flown in months—across the keys, writing and then deleting a sentence. I close my eyes, picturing the scene in my head.

"Belle," Nathaniel says, "I —"

I . . . what? Love your hair, babe? Your bonnet and homespun dress are fabulous? The last three years of celibacy have sucked? Wait, was that Nate speaking—or me?

It's time for a break. I pull my cat-eared slippers on, which I must have kicked off while writing, and pad out of my office toward the kitchen.

As I move, members of my sweet cat family shift and slip away from my moving feet, then sidle back, like silent, furry waves pooling around my ankles before receding back to the sea. I pick out Winston, Felix, and Lucky stalking my steps, while Sassy, Momo, and Milo lounge in a patch of sunlight in the living room. Others lie in their favorite spots on blankets along the backs of the leather couches or up on the dining room table. I *try* to keep them off the kitchen counters, but when you have as many cats as unshaved hairs on your legs, it's not easy.

Fluff is on the counter now, right smack in the middle of the cutting board. The whole counter is available, but no. She has to settle on the one piece of real estate where I prepare my food. I frown at her.

"You know you aren't supposed to be up here." She blinks at me with her gorgeous green eyes and I, of course, can't be mad. I lift her off and snuggle her. "I'm going to have fur in my lunch again, thanks to you."

She rubs her head against my chest, and I scratch between her ears, her favorite spot, then put her on the floor, where she twists around my leg and cries.

"Hungry?" I ask.

She answers with an emphatic meow. At least five others echo her. I check my watch. It's already noon. I'd sat down to write at around eight this morning and hadn't pulled my head out of my manuscript until now. If only I had more to show for it.

I walk into the pantry. On the right side is cat food. Stacks and stacks of cans plus several twenty-pound bags of kibble. On the left side, human food. Sandwich bread, bananas, nut butters, and some staples like rice and organic almond flour. I keep my reusable water bottle collection in here, and up top, on a shelf I have to reach on my tippy toes, a hidden stash of organic dark chocolate and candy.

It's definitely time for cinnamon bears.

Something about those pudgy red arms reaching out toward me, followed by the spicy sweetness on my tongue, kick starts my imagination while writing romantic scenes. There'd been no real-life inspiration lately, so . . . desperate times call for cinnamon bears.

I pull them down, along with the first aid kit. A little antibacterial spray and a Band-Aid, and my leg will be good as new. When I finish, a true crowd has gathered.

At least twenty cats of all shapes, sizes, colors, and patterns stare expectantly at me. Some make their desires known—from mewls to outright demands.

I wrangle several stacks of cans to the counter, blow aside fluffs of floating fur, and start opening, which prompts plenty of excited noises and pushing from the group around me. I keep cat food out for them, but when you have dozens of mouths to feed, the food runs low quickly. And keeping the cat litter clean is its own harrowing episode of *Dirty Jobs*.

While the cats jockey for position at the food bowls under the big bay window, I open the shades and peer outside for the first time today. I live along a two-lane highway up in the foothills near Boulder with few close neighbors, so it's super quiet. Exactly the way I like it. Aspen trees dance around my home and the sun is shining; I should go for a hike if I ever finish this scene.

And . . . after I write Aggie back. I have to accept her invitation, although I still have no idea what to say about my boyfriend.

Sucking on a squashy cinnamon bear, I sit back down at my desk and check my word count. Only fifteen hundred words written today. Usually in four hours I can get four thousand or more. I sigh and put my fingers back on the keyboard.

Finish this scene, Bea. Just this scene. The cursor blinks blankly at me.

I have to swallow my panic. Usually, I know what the hero would say. I can imagine. I can at least muddle through an answer. But lately, I don't *know*.

I walk back to the kitchen to boil water for my special anxiety blend tea, murmuring to the cats as I go. They normally soothe me, but I don't think it will be enough today. I pull out my favorite mug with a smiling tabby painted on it and perform the ritual of filling the kettle, pouring loose leaf tea in the diffuser, and waiting for the water to boil.

I check on Ever, the new foster kitten, as I wait. She's in the adjacent laundry room, which is one of the only rooms on the main floor that I can shut off so she won't be bothered by my other cats. I named her Ever because I got her in Evergreen. Not all that creative, but somehow the name fits her.

I've tried to give her some peace and quiet since I brought her home yesterday, but now I take her and my tea into my office and arrange a blanket for her. Fluff and Booboo stay close, along with about ten others, curious about their new housemate. Ever barely even looks around.

I open my household budget spreadsheet and review it again. My mortgage is reasonable thanks to a sizable down payment I put together from my strong book sales a few years ago, I don't eat much, and my hobbies aren't expensive. Hiking, taking drives in the mountains, occasionally eating out. I rarely go to the doctor.

But my cats, and CCR's rescue cats, are another story. Medical care, medications, food, and kitty litter for dozens and dozens of cats add up. Travis's fees are reasonable, but he has bills to pay, too. And my books definitely won't pay for Vilma and Robert's new facility.

Desperation creeps from my toes straight through the crown of my head. I need to finish this book, and I need to get my hands on my inheritance.

Feeling ridiculous, I open a tab in my browser, type in Boulder Craigslist, and slide the pointer to the Personals section. But after scanning the first few posts I reverse out of the page in a hurry. I'm about to close the tab when my eye pauses on another category: Boulder Activity Partners. I hesitate, and then click the link.

Most of the posts are people looking for innocent things like tennis partners, support group members, and even a gardening buddy. I lick my dry lips. Could this work?

Be brave, Saint Bea. Bea brave. Saint Bea is not brave. Saint Bea is a coward.

I swallow hard, and tears fill my eyes. Why am I like this? So afraid to do something new, out of the ordinary, something . . . a little risky.

If someone can find their next hockey team goalie on Craigslist, surely I can find a short-term business partner. Because that's all this would be—a business transaction.

I look down at Fluff and Ever to gather my courage, and then I type. Don't think, Bea-the-not-so-brave, just write.

Chapter Four

Sebastian

The coyote slinks forward through the grass, stalking a gray-brown rabbit. The rabbit's munching on mountain grass, completely unaware that in a matter of seconds, it could be freshly caught breakfast meat. I hold my breath as I shoot.

The rabbit freezes in my long-focus lens. Its nose twitches. The coyote pauses, waiting, probably willing its prey to go back to munching. I keep shooting.

The rabbit's nose twitches and a split-second later it shoots away. The coyote gives chase, its slim body rocketing across the field after it. For a second, I think it'll have its meal, but survival is stronger than hunger today. The rabbit disappears into the shelter of boulders tumbled across the hillside, and the coyote, after sniffing around for a few minutes, lopes away to find breakfast elsewhere.

I take my Canon off the tripod and look back through my shots. Some are worth editing. But even if they were all crap, it was a good morning's work. I stand, stretch, and pack up my equipment.

With the sun fully out, the Boulder foothills no longer look lit from within like they do right after sun up. Instead, everything is in Technicolor. The bluebird sky, lizard green grass and trees, and dusty brown rocks and dirt, set off by the cheerful reds, oranges, and yellows of a few patches of early summer wildflowers, are like a runny color palette. The valley's empty of other people, so far as I can tell. On early weekday mornings like this, I usually have the place to myself, which is how I like it.

I hike along the narrow and rocky dirt trail back to the main Walker Ranch hiking trail. Normally, I'd stay a little longer, wandering around and taking pictures of anything of interest, but there's an all-hands meeting at work in an hour. I'll just make it.

At the trailhead, I climb into Betty, my aging blue Bronco with her rusted sides and rumpled seats, and turn the key. *Click, click, click.* Uh oh. I twist the key back and forth, pump the gas pedal, and try again. Not even any clicks this time.

"Seriously, Betty? Today?" I would check the engine, but if it's a dead battery, no one is here to give me a jump. If it's not a dead battery, I won't have a clue how to fix it anyway.

I glance at my watch. I'm at least forty-five minutes from The Bitter, the lounge where I tend bar. That is, I *would* be forty-five minutes away if I had an operational vehicle.

I yank out my cell phone to call Triple A. Coverage here can be spotty, but thankfully I get through. They can be here in an hour. Given that Betty and I are stuck fairly deep in the foothills, that isn't bad, but I won't make it to the meeting.

I run a hand across Betty's faded dash. This might be it for her and me. A permanent breakup. My feeble bank account can't afford her anymore.

I pick out Evan's name from the favorites list on my phone. The cellular company takes a few seconds to think about whether or not I deserve to be connected after I was two weeks late paying last month's bill, but the call goes through. I can't miss the wary note in my bar manager's deep voice when he answers.

"Hey, Evan," I say, "listen, I'm really sorry, but I'm going to miss the meeting."

There's a long pause. "Second time this month, Seb."

"I know. I was shooting up at Walker Ranch this morning and my car broke down. I have to wait for a tow."

"There have only *been* two meetings this month, Seb."

I wince. "I'm sorry, man. I was planning to be there."

He doesn't speak for a second. I picture him smoothing his short, black hair and then his full beard, like he does when he's annoyed. "Your life's your business, but you might think about spending some of your next paycheck on a reliable vehicle."

"Usually, I bike to work—"

"Yeah, Seb, I know. But this is the second time this month your hobby got in the way of your employment. You get my point? I like you, and the customers like you, but you've got to get your priorities straight. Don't let this happen again."

I sigh, knowing he's right. "I won't."

"Okay, see you tonight. On time." The last two words were pointed.

Guilt squeezes my chest as I hang up. I'd worked at the Bitter Bar for eighteen months, and at a series of other joints around Boulder for the five years before that. After graduating from University of Colorado with a mostly useless degree in fine arts, specifically photography, I wasn't qualified to do much else.

I want to do a good job, but Evan's right. My heart isn't into mixing drinks and making conversation with boozy Boulderites until the wee hours. I loved being out here, with my camera. If I had my way, I'd be shooting, editing, and teaching photography. But Betty ate my money like bonbons and the rent had to be paid.

I text my roommate Javi to let him know where I am and settle in to wait. Triple A will tow Betty and me to the shop in

Boulder, and then I'll have to pay for a Lyft home to shower and change. At least I'll get to my shift.

My stomach rumbles like an angry cougar—which I'd actually heard once while on a shooting trip up in Montana. Scared the spit out of me. Keeping the door open for some fresh air, I pull a protein bar out of my jacket pocket and check my bank account app. This month will be dangerously tight.

A curious chipmunk shows up outside the car. Only a small bite of bar is left, but I break it into the tiniest pieces I can and scatter them in front of the little guy. I pull out my camera and shoot as the rodent sits on its haunches, holding a piece of food up to its comical front teeth before scampering to the next scrap. Maybe I can salvage the day and get a little money for these shots from Cheryl at Colorado Outdoors or at least on a stock photography website. It's not National Geographic, but it's something.

The munk takes off when the food's gone. Out of habit, I open the Craigslist app next. My finger strays toward the used camera equipment category. It's amazing what people will sell their perfectly good stuff for sometimes. I use a Canon 6D now. My dream is to find a 5D, what the pros use, for a steal. But today I resist even looking and browse used vehicles instead. *Very* used.

"Sorry, old girl," I tell Betty. "You know I love you." Selling her will hurt, but I don't think I have a choice. On the other hand, I don't see anything else I can easily afford. I save a few posts to look at again later, then, to kill time, open the Boulder Activity Partners link.

I check my post about the weekend photography hikes that I run for cheap. It's my side-side-hustle to make a little extra money. The small groups are usually a lot of fun, and I meet some interesting people. I even met my last girlfriend, Samantha, on one of the hikes. We dated for about six months until she moved back home to Chicago in January for a job. My post's still there, but no takers yet.

A new post catches my eye. *Hiking partner wanted. Must love cats.*

My mouth twists. Hiking with cats? What, like mountain lions? That would be a hike to remember. I click the link.

Single twenty-something woman looking for single twenty-something man for hiking adventures. Must like cats. Compensation possible. Urgent.

I scratch my scruffy chin and catch a whiff of myself. Yeah, a shower is mandatory. So, this woman wants a single hiking partner that likes cats. She's willing to pay, and for some reason, it's urgent. I shake my head. Boulder attracts some real freaks. Part of its charm, actually.

I reverse out of the post, then the app. Hesitate. Then open the app and her post again. *Compensation* snags in my brain. I lay my head back on the seat.

I like to hike. I like cats fine. I need cash.

After a minute, I type out a reply. And as I do, I'm sure about one thing.

I might really, really regret this.

Chapter Five

Beatrix

I stand across the street from the Look What the Cat Dragged In Cafe in downtown Boulder, nervously shifting my feet and adjusting my shirt over my leggings.

It's after ten, and I should already be in there. *He* should already be in there. Sebastian. Seb. The tenth guy who responded to my Craigslist post.

To be honest, I was shocked anyone answered. But after exchanging messages with a few of them, I realized I should have put the word *platonic* somewhere in the post. One asked me what I liked to wear while hiking; another came right out and asked for pictures of me wearing only my hiking boots. A third wanted pictures of my cats.

Um, no.

Seb's message was straightforward and didn't send up major creep flags, so I wrote him back. When our brief exchanges didn't end in him asking for pictures of my or my cats' private parts, or a screen shot of my bank account, I reluctantly set up a meeting.

But I'm still wondering how I ended up here.

I bite my lip, thinking hard about getting back in my car and heading home. After I use the bathroom at the UPS store behind me. I'm sweaty and shaky, and my stomach is cramping. I wish I could have brought Fluff with me, but for obvious safety reasons, you can't bring cats to a cat cafe.

My chin drops to my chest. This was a terrible idea.

A bus drives by, temporarily blocking my view of the cafe. It's open; I saw the new hostess unlock the door ten minutes ago. But no one had gone in yet. Not me, and not mystery-man Seb.

What if he doesn't show up at all? That makes me breathe even harder. I'd already put Aggie off once, but she'd written again this morning. Five words: *The party is next weekend.*

Not, *can you come?* Not, *is this a convenient time?* Only a summons. I clench my jaw and pull myself up straight. I have to do this for CCR and all those homeless cats.

I march into the street, envisioning how spectacular the adoption facility will be if my plan works. I'm so lost in the fantasy that I don't see the blood red Tesla racing straight for me.

When I finally do, my bladder spasms, and I freeze, waiting for the T symbol on the car's nose to tag me as its latest autopilot victim. But in that second, someone wraps an arm around me and jerks me back to sidewalk safety.

Adrenaline pours through me, and then drains when I realize I'm not squashed all over Walnut Street. I slump against the strong, definitely male chest and burst into tears. The guy holds me, patting my back every so often, as I blubber all over his shirt.

After a minute, I come back to my senses, dig a handkerchief out of my bag and take off my glasses to mop my face. The small crowd of gawkers around us instantly blurs.

The guy keeps a hand on my shoulder. "Are you okay?"

I still can't see him, but his voice is nice. Rich and unhurried. I blow my nose before answering, then wad up the wet cloth and stuff it back in my bag. Thankfully, by the time I get my glasses back on, the crowd is moving on to the next near-disaster.

My rescuer watches me, his worried brown eyes probably assessing my mental health. He's about my age, average height, with shaggy dark hair and almond skin, and he's slim, almost wiry. But what catches my eye is his tear-stained t-shirt. It's old, torn, and paint-stained, but it features a cat curled in an armchair. I'm wearing one of my cat t-shirts, too, a cat sitting peacefully at the end of a crescent moon.

My eyes meet the guy's, and my heart gives a funny lurch.

"Are you Sebastian Ross, by any chance?"

Chapter Six

✦❦✦

Sebastian

That was close. Too close. Like ridiculously close. This woman was almost road kill.

Now my t-shirt's wet, my heart's pounding, and she's staring at my chest. She asks in a tiny voice if my name is Sebastian.

I swallow and nod. "Beatrix?"

"Bea." She sniffs and pushes her glasses up the bridge of her petite nose. "I go by Bea. Beatrix is such a mouthful, you know?"

Beatrix is a cool name, but Bea is short and sweet—and seems to fit her. Everything about her is small. Small face, small, nicely put together body, and small feet. All the smallness makes her huge multi-colored eyes stand out that much more behind her glasses. Her left eye is blue and the right is hazel. They're sort of mesmerizing. I wish I had my camera.

Bea sees me staring, and she clutches her bag against her chest. "Thank you so much for pulling me out of the way. I'm an idiot for not looking where I'm going."

I smile. "I'm glad now that I was late."

She smiles, too, but doesn't meet my eyes. I can already tell that she's shy, like painfully. My curiosity grows.

"Do you still want to get a coffee?" I ask.

She throws a desperate look down the street toward a pay parking lot, and for a second I think she might make a break for her car, but then she pulls her shoulders back and nods.

I hold her elbow as we cross the street. She stiffens a little when I touch her, but it seems like the thing to do after she almost made herself into a hood ornament. For the record, her arm is tiny, too.

I open the door for her, and we step inside. Beyond a waist-high gate are couches, chairs, low tables, and in the back, a coffee bar. Soft indie music plays in the background. It's a standard cafe set up—except for all the cats.

They're everywhere, lying on furniture, spread out in patches of sun, and sitting by the bar. Every once in a while I hear a soft meow. The vibe is pretty chill.

A hostess checks us in. We have to sign waivers that we won't sue the place if we're scratched or bitten, and we have to pay by the half-hour or hour.

"Part of the entry fee goes to take care of our cats," the woman explains. "They're all rescues available for adoption. If you'd like to know more about any of them, please ask."

I reach for my wallet, but Bea beats me to it.

The barista, a woman with pink hair and plenty of piercings, greets Bea by name. We get our drinks—black coffee for me, tea with lemon for her—which I insist on paying for, then we sit on a couch by a window. Bea immediately moves closer to the resident cat, a big orange one with markings like an M on its forehead, and tugs it into her lap. The cat kneads Bea's leggings once or twice, and then curls up. She scratches the cat, seeming to know exactly what to do to make it purr.

"Do you come here a lot?" I ask.

She nods and shrugs. "It's kind of my home away from home."

She doesn't say anything else, so I sip my coffee and wait. This is her show. She keeps scratching the cat for a minute, and I get the sense she's working up to whatever it is she has to say. But all she does is get a little pink in her pale cheeks. The silence is getting awkward. Maybe she needs some help getting started.

"So, you're looking for a hiking partner," I say.

Her cheeks grow redder. "Do you like to hike?"

"Love it. I hike most mornings, although it's usually to get to a better spot to shoot from."

She grimaces. "Shoot? You . . . hunt?" She cradles the cat for a second, like she thinks I might whip a knife out right there and skin it.

I hold my hands up. "No, I'm a photographer. I shoot pictures—wildlife and nature."

She settles back against the couch and releases the cat, who looks annoyed. "Oh. Oh, that's cool. Do you freelance for magazines or something?"

"I've sold a few images." Literally a few. "I'm still working on my portfolio." I've edited thousands of images the last few years, but I'm never quite happy with them.

"So what do you do for work?" she asks.

"I'm a bartender at the Bitter," I say. She looks blank. "It's a bar. We have a great patio and happy hours on Fridays and Saturdays. You should come by. Do you live in town?"

She shakes her head. "I'm up in Coal Creek Canyon."

"Nice. It's beautiful back there." A little far away, maybe, but beautiful. "Do you have roommates?"

She laughs, showing rows of even white teeth, and I realize it's the first time I've seen her really grin. It lights up her pretty face.

"Yeah, a bunch." She sounds like the joke is on me.

I smile. "So what's all this about, Bea?"

Chapter Seven

Beatrix

I sip my tea before I answer, fighting the urge to hide under the couch cushions.

So far, Seb seems normal. Nice even. He insisted on paying for our drinks and he's being very patient with me. Not to mention preventing me from becoming road kill. And . . . he's good looking. Cuter than I had any right to expect. Not that it matters. Anyway, I can't put off explaining my bizarre post any longer.

"I have . . . a confession. And a problem." I scratch MacTavish, the cat on my lap. I know him—and all these cats—well. I come here twice a week to write when I need a change of scenery. I've even adopted a few of the cafe's cats when they couldn't find homes for them. The hostess is new, which is why she didn't recognize me like the barista, Quinn, did.

Seb waits on me to say more. His lips curve into a smile, which I can't help but notice is kind of sexy. He has a thin nose and one of those lantern jaws where the bones in the back show prominently, giving him an aristocratic kind of look. At least the way aristocrats look on the cover of Regency romances.

"The hiking thing was . . . kind of a ruse," I tell him. "I do like to hike, but I usually go on my own. What I need is . . . a fiancé."

Chapter Eight

Sebastian

A fiancé? My thoughts scramble.

"You want . . . a husband?" I ask.

She makes a face. "No!"

"Then I don't understand."

She turns toward me. The cat in her lap cracks open a golden eye and slowly unfurls the claws on its front paws. I have a feeling it will let Bea know if she does something it doesn't like.

"What I need is a *fake* fiancé. To present to my father. He's older and annoyingly patriarchal. He wants to be sure I'm taken care of before he . . . in case anything happens to him." She shrugs. "I've made it clear that I don't need a man to take care of me, but he doesn't agree."

"What do you need this fake fiancé to do?" I ask.

Bea speaks quickly, as if she has to or the words won't come out at all. "Here's my idea. I'll pay you to spend time with me— maybe hiking, maybe something else—"

My eyes happen to be on her glossed lips as she says that. I swear it was a coincidence, but she falters, and then hurries on again.

"So we learn enough about each other to get through a four-day visit with my family. My father's turning eighty, and my sister is having a birthday party for him."

"Where do they live?"

"On a ranch up near Aspen."

Aspen—a gorgeous area for hiking, mountain biking, skiing in the winter, and shooting. The idea suddenly sounds more intriguing.

Bea goes on. "I know this is a lot to ask. You'll have to spend time with me over the next week and then take off of work when we go to Aspen. But I can pay you for your time and expenses."

She sounds like spending time with her is something that someone would *need* to be paid to do. So far, I think I'd like spending time with her. She's quirky but in a sweet way. And I'd seen flashes of spirit, too.

I put my mug down. "Bea, don't you have a, well, a friend you can ask?"

Her face goes furiously red, and I realize I've touched a nerve. Even the cat feels it. Its eyes pop open with alarm.

"I want to keep this professional." She pulls an envelope out of her bag and hands it to me. "You'll find my terms are generous."

The piece of paper inside has a contract typed out on it. Two weeks of work for—my jaw drops, and I meet Bea's steady gaze. "What do *you* do for a living?"

She ignores my question. "I'll pay half at our first meeting, then half after the four days with my family. And there's a potential for a bonus, if you try your best to convince my father that we'll be blissfully happy together. But I want to be clear about something, Seb. This is a business arrangement. I'm not looking for a hook up or romance, and I hope you're not, either."

I smile. "Bea, I was only looking for a hiking partner who

likes cats." *And who's willing to pay cash,* I think, with an ounce of shame.

She's all business now. "I have one more term I'd like you to agree to. What's your most prized possession?"

"My camera." I answer without thinking but then narrow my eyes. "Why?"

"I want you to agree, in writing, that we will keep things professional . . . or you'll give up your camera."

I laugh. She's obviously joking. Wait—she's not. "You're serious."

"Absolutely."

With any thoughts brewing about the possible perks of getting to know Bea better suddenly squashed, I shrug. "I can agree to that. What about you? What's your prized possession?"

"My cats."

No surprise there, I guess. "So you're agreeing to give one up?" I'm teasing her, but her eyes widen and she pales. I'm not sure that was what she had in mind.

"I was going to give up my practically brand new laptop. Which I really need. But . . . okay." She lifts her chin. "If I treat you in any way other than as a colleague, I will give up one of my cats."

"Which one? I mean, I think this should go in the contract." I'm still kidding around, but she's taking it seriously.

Bea's eyes dart around the room in that way again, like she might bolt. When her legs start to bounce up and down, the cat jumps off her lap in a huff and stalks off. I suddenly feel like Rumplestiltskin asking her to contractually give up her first born.

"I'm joking," I say. "You don't—"

"Fluffernutter, my tuxedo cat. I'll add it to the contract."

Looking kind of nauseated, she writes *camera* and *Fluff* on the contract with a shaky hand.

"Does this mean you're interested in the job?" she asks.

I cock my head. "One more question . . . aren't you taking

this a little far with your father? Can't you tell him you don't need a husband? Or find some other way to convince him?"

She bites her lower lip. "There's this inheritance money. I need it to help fund a worthy cause—a cat rescue and adoption facility that one of my favorite charities is building—but Dad won't pass it on to me until I'm *settled*."

I drum my fingers on my knees. Bea's an odd girl, and this has to be the strangest interview I've ever had, but at least her motivation makes sense. We're both in this for the money, although she'll use hers for a much more altruistic purpose than I will.

Anyway, I'd had worse jobs. Like the time my friend and I had the brilliant idea to start a dog poop pickup business in high school but had no way to transport the massive bags of poop other than the back of my mom's SUV. After an accidental tear in one of the bags, the smell lingered for *years*.

"Okay." I hold out my hand for the pen. "Where do I sign?"

Chapter Nine

Sebastian

I tell Javi about my new side hustle over takeout at our apartment that night. After he stops laughing, he asks me why I agreed to Bea's nutty deal.

"Did I mention the money?"

He raises a thick, black eyebrow. "You could work a few months of extra shifts to make enough to fix Betty." He shifts his rice noodles around his bowl. "Is it the girl?"

Is it?

"No, that's not happening." I describe the provision about Bea and me giving up our most prized possessions if we get involved.

"That's so dramatic." He pauses with his chopsticks full of dripping noodles and veggies halfway to his mouth. "You could always buy another camera."

"I saved for a year to get my 6D. I'm not giving it up, unless I trade it for a 5D." And somehow, I don't think Bea would see one of her cats as replaceable, either.

But the whole drive up Coal Creek Canyon to her house, a drive I'm making on my one day off this week so I can get to know a stranger well enough to trick her own family, I ponder Javi's original question. Why am I doing this again?

Betty coughs and sputters every time I downshift, and I remember. Money. It's about the money. The mechanic had gotten Betty moving again, but he charged a fortune and didn't make any promises about how long it would be before the next repair.

The road up through the canyon is twisty with rock walls on either side. It follows a swirling stream flowing the opposite direction. Framed by the blue sky, it's a beautiful drive, but . . . Bea's house is way back in here. She had to send me a dropped pin on Google because she said mapping her address didn't always get you to the right spot. How did she persuade all those roommates to live so far out of town? Most of my friends and coworkers want to live as close to Boulder or Denver as they can afford to.

I pull off the main road onto a narrow gravel road. It winds up into the woods, ending in a circle in front of a large two-story mountain home made of wood beams and glass. A Prius and a Range Rover sit outside. Bea's other roommates must be at work.

I climb out of Betty and look around. The trees rustle around the house, birds chirp, and I spot a narrow hiking trail behind the house, heading up the hill. The air smells piney and clean up here, like it's freshly scrubbed.

I ring the doorbell. Something scurries behind the door. Make that lots of somethings, from the sound of it. I step back. The door opens after a minute, and Bea slips out. Her brown hair, in a ponytail today, glistens in the sun. She's wearing slim fitting jeans and a green short-sleeved blouse with small white cat outlines all over it. The color brings out the interesting hazel in her right eye. She's barefoot, and her toenails are painted.

"Thanks for coming." She pushes her glasses up her nose

with her pointer finger. I noticed at our first meeting that she wrinkles her nose when she does that; it's cute. "Before we go in, I should tell you something."

"Okay." I shove my hands in the pockets of my shorts, wondering why we can't discuss whatever it is inside instead of on the porch.

"I like cats," she says.

"I know, Bea."

She licks her lips and threads her hands together in front of her. "I mean I *really* like them. I've adopted a lot of rescue cats over the last few years." Something scratches at the door behind her and then thumps. Bea turns an ear that way, seeming to listen to whatever's going on in there.

"How many cats are we talking about?" I ask.

She eyes me. "You'll see. Move slowly at first, and let them get used to you. Some will hide, but others like to guard the house, and . . . they aren't used to many guests." She fidgets and looks away as she says the last part. She turns to open the door, but half-turns back. "Oh, and sorry about the smell."

With that, she opens the door and we go in. She closes it quickly behind me. It's darker inside, so it takes my eyes a minute to adjust, but I can hear the cats moving around me.

Ahead of us, the entryway leads into a two-story great room with a huge stone fireplace, comfortable-looking leather couches, and a massive dining room table. A hallway leads off to the left, which is also where the garage was, so I'm guessing the kitchen is to the right. The walls are white, the classy furniture is neutral colors, and there are green plants everywhere.

I wonder again what Bea does for a living, but I'm distracted from my thoughts by the smell: used kitty litter, and lots of it. I switch to breathing through my mouth. And I finally notice all the cats.

They're *everywhere*. On the couches, the chairs, the table, and slinking behind furniture. One climbs curtains by the dining table window, and another lies on the rod at the top. A few more peek out from under blankets.

I try to count them, but stop when I get over twenty. They're moving around too much to keep track of anyway. They're big, small, white, black, orange, brown, and gray, some all one color, and others with markings. And these aren't all of them; Bea said some would hide. My mouth hangs open.

"How many cats do you actually have?"

Her pale cheeks go pink. "A lot. I haven't counted in a while."

I gaze around again. I see plenty of cats, but no signs of other humans. Like jackets hanging on things, shoes kicked by the back door, discarded bags or backpacks, that kind of thing. And I realize—when Bea said she had a lot of roommates, she meant her cats.

She's . . . a cat lady.

Seriously, what am I doing here again?

Chapter Ten

Beatrix

Seb stares around at my home, studies my cats, and then studies me. He looks like he can't decide whether to laugh or call for a mental health welfare check.

I hope he can't tell, but I'm sweating through my blouse. I cross my arms and swallow against the knot in my throat. My cats aren't the only one unused to having guests. And I hate feeling judged in my own home.

Why can't I be breezy and confident? Raise a challenging eyebrow and dare him to criticize how I choose to live? So I care for a large number of homeless cats, I should say. So what?

Instead, I'm frozen, my mouth is dry, and I can't think of a single thing to say. I feel the panic rising. When Seb bolts forward toward the couch, I jump back, half-reaching for the pepper spray I tucked in my pocket just in case. Then I realize what he's doing.

Poor old Jinx likes to sleep on the back of the couch, but sometimes he sleeps so deeply that he rolls right off. Seb catches him before he hits the ground and cradles him against his chest. Jinx blinks with surprise, like *how did I end up here?* His tail flicks, and his eyes close again. Back to sleep.

Seb and I look at each other. When he laughs, the strangling tightness in my chest gives way.

"That's Jinx, one of my old men. You can put him down on that cushion if you want." I gesture to a cat cushion I bought especially for the older folks. Seb sets him down carefully. I point to a few other cats. "This is Sassy, Callie, and Tiger. Midnight and Jazz are over there."

I stop. He's looking freaked out again as more of my cats creep in from other rooms, curious about the new human. Finally, my mother's lessons in being a good hostess come back to me.

"Would you like something to drink?" I ask. "I have tea, coffee, homemade kombucha, or I made a pitcher of fruit-infused water."

"Water is great."

I lead him into the kitchen, pour two glasses, and pull a small tray of olives, crackers, and hummus out of the fridge. He takes the tray, I take the water glasses, and after I shoo Oreo off the table, Seb and I sit.

Cats circle around our chairs, their unblinking gazes on Seb. Nicky, my stocky British shorthair, twitches her tail ever so slightly. Uh oh. I keep an eye on her.

"So to start," I say, "I should probably tell you about—"

Three things happen at the same time. Nicky launches herself onto the table, a blast of compressed air goes off, and startled, Seb jerks back in his chair, falling and banging his head on the ground.

I jump up and lean over him. "I'm so sorry. Are you okay?"

"I think so." He lifts his head and winces. Nicky sits on Seb's empty plate, watching her work with satisfaction.

I take Seb's hand to help him, and a tingly feeling runs

between our fingers, up my arm, and jolts wildly around my stomach for a few seconds before shooting to my knees.

I blink. I haven't felt that kind of electrical shock in a long time. I'm not sure what it is, but I know what it's not.

It's not attraction. Not at all.

Really, it's true.

Chapter Eleven

Sebastian

Ouch.

A cat launched itself at me and now I'm on my back, staring at my knees and the kitchen ceiling beyond. My head throbs from hitting the kitchen floor so hard.

Bea leans over me, her expression horrified. Her mesmerizing eyes distract me from the pain, and I suddenly notice her delicious scent, like salt and limes.

"Are you all right?" she asks.

I'm not totally sure since I smell citrus fruits and all, but I say I'm okay. Bea helps me up. Her soft hand sends a sharp current through my arm and straight to my gut.

"What was that?" I mean what had attacked me, but the double meaning seems glaring.

"*That,*" she frowns at the cat on my plate, "is Nicky. And that," she points to the container of compressed air, "is my attempt to keep the cats off the table. It works better for some than others. Most of them have learned to jump on a part of the table that doesn't trigger the air. Nicky just doesn't care."

Bea pulls her hand out of mine. I didn't realize I was still holding it. She plucks Nicky off the table and sets her on the ground where the cat saunters away like *my job here is done.*

"Are you sure you're all right?" Bea asks.

I tell her I am, and to show her, right my chair and sit again. I put some snacks on my plate and try to surreptitiously fish a little cat hair out of my water before taking a drink.

Bea makes a face. "Sorry. Cat hair is a constant environmental hazard in this house."

I wave it off. "What were you going to tell me before Nicky, er, introduced herself?"

She puts two olives, two crackers, and a small dollop of hummus on her plate. She might love cats, but she eats like a bird.

"That I'm vegan. My diet will come up with my family. They all eat meat."

"Vegan, huh? So what do you like?"

"A lot of salads, rice bowls, and I love all kinds of Asian food. I like tea with lemon, I don't drink coffee, and white wine is my vice."

It's good to know she has one with all that healthy eating. I pull a notepad and pen from my back pocket and start writing. She chews an olive and watches me.

I lift the pad. "Taking notes to study later."

She looks pleased, which, inexplicably, pleases me.

"What about you?" she asks. "What kinds of foods do you like?"

"I'm a carnivore, I'm afraid." I try to look sorry, but I don't think I quite pull it off. "I like steak, I drink black coffee because it's easy and cheap, and I can't resist a good whiskey if someone's buying. As for vices, I don't smoke or do drugs, and I do a lot of hiking and mountain biking, so I don't know . . . I don't eat enough greens?"

She smiles. "How old are you, Seb?"

"Twenty-seven. You?"

"Twenty-eight."

"You're robbing the cradle with me, then." I look around the kitchen at her newish appliances, quartz countertops, and the large pantry. Our apartment could fit in this one room with space to spare. "What do you do for work?" I asked her at the cat cafe, but she didn't answer.

She squirms in her chair. "I write books."

"Yeah? What kind?" And why does she look embarrassed about it?

"Romances."

My smile gets wider. "Seriously? Like the hot and steamy kind? With those bare chested dudes on the covers?"

She rolls her eyes. "All kinds. Sweet, steamy, and everything in-between. I'm writing a sweet Western series now, but my last was contemporary romantic comedy."

I wrangle my smile back under control. She's sensitive about her work. Well, I understand that. Every time my friend Jayden sees one of my images, he acts like he could have taken it with his iPhone. Pisses me off.

"Can I see one of your books?" I ask.

"Sure." She stands and points to a white cat at my feet. "Don't let Callie get on the table. She likes hummus."

Bea leaves for a couple of minutes. About half the cats follow her while the other half seem to be assigned to watching me.

When Bea returns, she hands me several books. Some do have those half-naked guys on them. One has a girl and guy, fully clothed, smiling at each other. One looks like fantasy or something; smoke and fire surrounds the bare-chested guy and leather-clad girl on the cover. None of them look like Westerns.

"What's your new one called? The one you're writing?" I ask.

"I'm never sure until I finish writing, but the tentative title is *The Long Trail to Love*."

I flip through one of the books, wondering how much of Bea

is in them. To be honest, she looks more like a travel writer or cat care blogger.

"Why romance?" I ask. "I mean, what do you like about writing it?"

She strokes a black and white cat that jumped into her lap. "I read romances growing up. I started sneaking them out of my mother's library when I was twelve. I found out later that she knew all along. She'd hide the sexier titles and put her favorite sweet romances where they were easier for me to find."

She looks out the window, her smile sad. "As I got older, she gave me others she thought I'd be ready for. And hid a few she never *wanted* me to be ready for."

"Will she be in Aspen when we go?"

She shakes her head. "Mom died five years ago."

"Ah—that sucks, Bea."

She takes her glasses off and wipes her eyes with a napkin. I don't see my parents that often right now, but that's not the same as not having them at all. I take her hand and squeeze it.

She squeezes back . . . and that zingy electrical current runs through me again. It feels like the time I stuck a fork in a wall socket in second grade. The shock made me cry, then. Today, it makes me want more.

Bea glances behind her and jumps to her feet. "Callie, no!"

The white cat is on the counter shredding a kitchen towel that had been hanging by the sink.

"Living here must be exhausting," I joke.

Bea smiles tiredly. "I can't leave much of anything out. Everyone has their favorite things to eat, sit on, or destroy." She collects up the books. "Let me put these away, and then it's your turn. I want to know about your job, your family, where you're from."

I get the feeling Bea doesn't like talking about herself that much. But if we're going to pull this scam off, she'll have to tell me all about herself very soon.

And the truth is that I'm starting to look forward to it, quirks and all.

Chapter Twelve

Beatrix

After the meeting at my house, where Seb was attacked, forced to check out my romance books, and had his hummus eaten by Callie, I'd visited Seb's apartment a few days later and met his roommate. Javi had an amused look on his face the whole time, so I figured Seb had told him about our contract. I would probably smirk too.

Seb showed me pictures of his older brother Jacob, and his parents, Mason and Jenna. They all live in Durango, where Seb grew up. His father's a marketing entrepreneur. His mom works for the town's planning department. They're avid hikers and skiers.

Seb and I had shared a lot with each other over the last week. I felt like we knew enough to pull this scam off—maybe. But it was all factual, surface stuff. I didn't tell him everything. Real couples don't share every single personal thing, do they?

Anyway, ready or not, Seb and I are heading to Aspen the day after tomorrow. I'd contacted Gail, my longtime cat sitter, and scheduled her for the days I'd be away. She was the only person I'd found who was willing to stay with all my cats. She agreed to keep a close eye on Ever.

Travis put Ever on an antibiotic, which perked her up a little. But she still isn't eating, drinking, or exploring as much as I'd hoped she'd be by now. I wish I could bring her with me, but it's better to leave her here with Gail. My family could stress out a tree stump.

I walk out to my back deck with a cup of green tea to soak up the summer sun and enjoy the quiet before calling Aggie. She picks up after one ring.

"Beatrix—it's about time you called. Father's been asking about you every day. Are you still coming?"

I sigh. Aggie sounds so much like Mom as she gets older. But they were nothing alike.

"Hey, nice to talk to you, too," I say to make a point. "How have you been?"

"Fine." Aggie's voice is clipped. "The twins are sick, Dad's been in a mood, and Ben had to go to Denver all week for work, but I can handle it."

Of course she can. Aggie can handle everything. She always has.

"I'm sorry the twins are sick. What's going on with them?"

"It's a virus. Dr. Wright checked them out yesterday."

Aggie and her husband Ben's twins, Kate and William, are eight. They were born on the sixteenth of November 2010, the day the British royals got engaged. Mom passed her love for all things British on to Aggie. If Aggie had another set of girl-boy twins, I wouldn't be surprised if she called them Meghan and Harry.

"So? Are you coming?" She sounds impatient.

Last chance. I could say I'm not coming. Or that I'm coming alone. I can find another way to fund the facility. I should be honest. But since when has the Fuller family ever been honest with each other?

"We'll be there Sunday afternoon," I say.

"And your boyfriend? What's his name again?"

"Sebastian."

She's quiet. "That's his name? That's not what I thought you told me."

I squirm in my seat. I'd told each of my family members a different fictional-boyfriend name the past few years, knowing no one was paying enough attention to be certain.

"Aggie, I know my own boyfriend's name. And, while we're on the subject, Seb's my fiancé now."

"Really." My sister sounds surprised—and suspicious. "Since when?"

"Since this past weekend." Seb and I had already agreed on the details of our fake engagement story. He'd whisked me away to San Francisco for the weekend and proposed while gazing out at the Golden Gate Bridge, the sun kissing our cheeks, and the wind blowing our hair back. It was so romantic; it still gives me fake chills.

"Well. Congratulations, Beatrix."

"Thanks, Ag." She especially hates it when I call her that.

"I'll tell Father, then, shall I? And we'll get one of the guest rooms ready for you two at the house."

One guest room. One—for Seb and me. I groan internally. I'll deal with the awkwardness of *that* situation later.

"Thanks, Aggie. We'll see you soon."

I hang up the phone, sip my tea, and mentally prepare to face my family.

Let the games begin.

Chapter Thirteen

Sebastian

Bea and I are about half an hour outside of Aspen, cruising past the little town of Basalt. She insisted on driving, which was probably for the best because, well, Betty. And the three-and-a-half hour drive gave us a little more time to cram.

I frame shots of the sprawling mountain range in my head, the peaks and valleys, the surprising patches of wildflowers, the winding stream I catch glimpses of from the two-lane highway. If I were alone, I'd stop to take a few pictures.

Instead, notebook in hand, I quiz Bea. I knew a lot about her after the last week, but it was like reading a Wikipedia version of her life. I wasn't too sure I knew the whole story.

"Childhood friends?" I ask.

"Nora and Jess. Nora still lives in the valley, but Jess moved to Northern California."

I'd figured out "the valley" meant the Roaring Fork Valley, where Aspen is located. "Best subject in school?"

She glances at me, eyebrow raised. *English*, I write in my book.

"Favorite teacher?"

She smiles. "Ms. McLeod, first grade. She had white, puffy, hair, like a cloud, and she handed out lollypops on Friday afternoons. Looking back, I think it was to shut us up for the last half-hour of the week when her nerves were frayed."

I scratch out notes, careful not to get pen marks on my clothes. I'm wearing my nicest jeans, a collared shirt, and I have a vest ready to throw on. Bea said her family wasn't that formal, but this is Aspen.

Growing up in low-key Durango, we'd joked about Aspen with all its billionaires. *You know what you call two skiers drinking champagne and having sex on the slopes? Aspenites.*

I click the end of the pen several times. Now that the visit with Bea's family is officially here, I'm nervous. First, I'm not rich. Far from it. I barely own my car. Second, I doubt I'm what her family is hoping for and their disapproval could make for a pretty uncomfortable week. Not that it matters, since this is all a sham. And finally, this is all a sham. What happens if I screw up and they find me out?

A meow comes from the backseat, distracting me from my thoughts. I turn around. "You all right back there, Fluffernutter?"

The black and white cat gazes at me from the cat carrier. I didn't ask Bea why she brought Fluff or what her family would think. Lots of people brought their dogs when they visited family, so why not a cat? At least she didn't bring all of them.

I study Bea out of the corner of my eye. Today she has on a thin sweater with jeans and boots. No cat clothes in sight. Her hair is down around her shoulders. The ends are blowing in the slight breeze from the cracked windows. I want to touch her hair, feel if it's as soft as it looks.

She looks relaxed at the moment, but I can tell she's as nervous as I am. She's a funny girl. One minute she can be confident and self-assured, the next minute she seems a little lost in her life.

"What kind of music do you like?" she asks me.

"All kinds, but rap and hip hop are probably my favorites. You?"

She gives me a sideways glance. "Don't laugh . . . country."

I do laugh. She doesn't seem like the type. "Seriously?"

"I grew up listening to it with friends; there are a lot of ranching people in the valley. It's officially country *and* western music, you know. I loved Faith Hill, Lady Antebellum, some Blake Shelton, and few of the classics like Merle Haggard, Waylon Jennings, and Patsy Cline. It drove my parents nuts." Her smile at the memory is short lived. "But I like pop and hip hop, too. Love Beyoncé and Cardi B, and Childish Gambino is crazy talented."

"Well at least we can plan our wedding playlist now," I say. "Speaking of, when and where are we tying the knot?"

Her shoulders droop. "Can we say we haven't decided? I don't think I can deal with fake wedding planning right now."

"Sure. But so you know, I've always wanted a destination wedding. Like a beach in Costa Rica followed by scuba diving in Belize on our honeymoon. Or maybe Barcelona and then hiking around Spain."

"You have expensive taste." She laughs, which was always satisfying; her laughs were rare.

I put an arm behind her seat. "Yeah, but I've got a sugar mama."

She freezes, and her knuckles go white on the wheel. "Don't call me that."

I blink. I was completely teasing. I'd never expect any fiancée —fake or real—to fund our wedding and honeymoon. "Okay. Sorry, Bea."

She loosens her grip and sighs. "No, *I'm* sorry."

I hesitate. I could tell there were a few things she didn't want to talk about. Her mom was one. Her obsession with cats was another. This felt like a new one.

She doesn't say anything for a minute. "You should probably know about this because it could come up with my family . . . I had a serious relationship a few years ago. We were engaged for a while, but we broke up."

She'd been engaged? I feel sort of disappointed. Don't be stupid, Seb.

She went on. "We went to high school together, and he was a great student, sporty, popular. His parents weren't wealthy, and I think he always felt insecure because they couldn't afford to live in town, and he had to have part-time jobs and everything. But I always felt like *he* was out of *my* league. When we started dating seriously senior year in college, people—including my own family —whispered he was with me for my money. I ignored them, but a few things happened and . . . anyway. After we broke up, I wondered if the whispers were true. If I was his sugar mama after all."

She shrinks in her seat, looking for a second like she might break into pieces.

I touch her hand. "I really am sorry, Bea. I didn't know."

She throws me a smile. "Breakups suck, right?"

"Yeah, let's never break up. Since we aren't actually together, shouldn't be hard to do."

"We might be on to something here. Having a fake relationship means a no break-up guarantee."

We laugh, and I realize I laugh with her a lot. Even though we haven't known each other for long, and our romantic relationship is a farce, we feel like friends. Bea doesn't seem to have many friends. I'm not sure why, other than that people seem to make her uncomfortable, which I guess is a pretty good reason.

We're in downtown Aspen now. It's a mix of modern and Victorian buildings, shops, homes, fancy hotels and restaurants, and of course the ski mountain, which is turning summer green. I'd been to Aspen a handful of times to hike and camp since college but never to ski. Too pricey. It was bad enough at Vail or Breckenridge, where I had a local discount pass the winters I could afford one.

Bea told me her dad's home is about ten minutes past town. As we drive on, she taps her fingers on the wheel.

"You okay?" I ask.

She nods and then gifts me with a genuine smile. "Thank you for doing this, Seb. I know I'm paying you for your time, but I'm so grateful for your help."

"You're welcome." I don't love it when she reminds me she's paying me. It makes me feel like an escort or something. If we'd been friends first, I would have come to Aspen for free. But the fact is that my bank account's already breathing a sigh of relief from Bea's initial, more-than-generous payment.

I tug at her sleeve. "Don't worry. We've got this. Your family will buy our story by the time we leave, your dad will feel better, shower you with riches, and you can break up with me."

"I hope you're right."

I snort. "That eager to ditch me?"

She pulls a face. "Yeah, you're kind of a pain."

I clutch my chest. "Ouch, that hurts, Bea. You're a hard woman to please."

"You bet I am. And don't forget it."

Ha. I got her to smile again.

We pull off the highway that continues up to Independence Pass and turn onto what looks like a long driveway, following it up a hill through some trees. To our right is the ridge that Aspen Mountain is part of, and behind us is the valley, which has been narrowing as we've gone along.

After a while, the driveway opens up to a long stretch of grass and a paved circle beside a freaking enormous house. I stare at it. This monster has to be more than five thousand square feet. It sits at an angle, so as we drive up, I can see a bit of both sides of the house. At the front, a long porch with comfortable-looking seating faces the ridge. A huge covered patio at the back of the house peers over the town of Aspen and the valley. The backyard has cut grass and some landscaping with native evergreens, aspens, and beds of flowers that my mom could probably easily name.

I knew Bea's family had money, but this is next level rich.

Bea parks in the circle and switches the car off but doesn't move to get out. She takes a long, unsteady breath.

"I can do this." She mutters to herself before turning to me. "Ready?"

"Ready. One adoring and adorable fake fiancé coming right up." I hold up a hand for her to high-five.

Instead, she places her palm gently against mine with a watery smile.

And, damn. It feels good.

Chapter Fourteen

Beatrix

I take Fluff and her carrier out of the car, Seb gets our bags, and we walk to the door. I have a key, but I ring the doorbell instead, embarrassed to have Seb see how shaky I would be while trying to insert the key into the lock.

He smiles at me, looking relaxed and confident. I meant what I said; I'm so grateful he's here. Something about being with Seb puts me at ease. It doesn't hurt that he's hot as an extra-spicy cinnamon bear, either. His hair—wavy, dark, and begging to be stroked—frames his face, and something about the way he moves, at ease in his own body, draws my eye. He made an effort to shave and dress up a little, too, which I appreciate since my family will be inspecting him like a prize-winning steer at the county fair. I face the door and slap on a smile as it opens.

"Aunt Beatrix! You're here! Will, tell them she's here!" Kate stands at the door, hopping up and down, while her twin brother tears back into the house to announce our arrival. I relax when I see it's her.

"Hey Katydid, come give me a hug." I set Fluff's carrier down and hold out my arms for Kate to charge into. "How are you feeling?"

"I'm fine, but Will still has a runny nose, and he keeps wiping it on me."

"Yuck," I say. "Uncle Henry used to do the same thing to me."

My petite, blonde, and blue-eyed niece is wearing a ruffled dress entirely inappropriate for the changeable mountain weather—probably Aggie's doing. But I'm happy to see Kate's hair is a wreck, as if my sister couldn't convince, cajole, or command her daughter to brush it out. I used to have similar rebellions as a girl when Aggie tried to boss me around. Kate clutches me for a second but then turns to Fluff.

"You brought Fluff! Can I take her out?" she asks.

"Yes, but be careful with her. Remember, she's little and can't handle a lot of roughhousing."

"I'll remember." She pulls Fluff out, tucks her in her arms, and runs after her brother. "Will, Sienna—Aunt Bea brought Fluff! Come see!"

"Wait, you didn't meet Sebastian . . ." My voice trails off, and I shrug apologetically at him. "That was Kate. Sorry, you don't rate as highly as Fluff."

"Course not," he says.

We're still standing on the porch because I can't bring myself to step inside. The house, the property, even the *smell* of home— a mixture of vanilla candles, wood smoke, and crisp mountain air —reminds me of Mom. She would have greeted us at the door, if she were still here. My heart spasms.

"Are you all right?" Seb's eyebrows pinch together with concern.

He doesn't miss much, does he? I'm not all that okay, but we spent the last week and a half preparing for this. I can't chicken out now. I square up to the door and walk in—a good soldier marching into battle.

I only hope we survive the war.

Chapter Fifteen

Sebastian

A blonde woman meets us in the doorway. Her eyes are big, like Bea's, but she's a lot taller, and her hair is longer. Still, this has to be Bea's sister.

Bea holds out her arms as if to hug Aggie, but her sister kisses Bea's cheeks instead, and Bea's smile fades. Aggie's expression is a little frosty as she greets me.

"Very nice to meet you, Sebastian."

I can feel Aggie examining me as I step inside, so I keep smiling. She gestures to an out of the way corner of the sunny, two-story entryway. "You can leave your bags here and collect them later. Please, come in."

Bea told me that although Aggie, her husband Ben, and their twins live on a property a few miles away from here, Aggie manages her father's home and her own, some of their real estate investments, and she's on the board of their family's charitable organization, the Fuller Family Foundation. And according to Bea, she does it all perfectly.

I set the bags down, and Aggie leads us from the entry to the massive combined kitchen and family room. With high ceilings, lots of square footage, and tons of wood, natural stone, and expensive-looking textiles, the place is as grand on the inside as it is on the outside. I feel like I should pay my couple of bucks, take pictures, and move on out with the rest of the riffraff.

The family is gathered in the great room, sitting on the massive leather sectional and assorted chairs as we come in. I take Bea's hand. We're newly engaged, after all, so it seems like the thing to do. She stiffens but luckily isn't shocked enough to yank her hand away.

Everyone stands, and an older man comes forward. He's tall and lean, like Aggie, with a full head of white hair and whiskery eyebrows. He limps slightly; Bea said he has rheumatoid arthritis along with a few other health issues. But even at eighty, he still looks like he could take down a bear or wrestle an alligator with ease. Or at least bully a table full of executives.

"Beatrix, you're here. Finally." The word finally doesn't sound like: *You're finally here! I missed you*. It's sounds like: *You finally obeyed my orders*. He opens his arms and Bea steps into them hesitantly, as if she wonders if instead of getting a hug, she's walking into a trap.

"Dad, I'd like you to meet my fiancé, Sebastian Ross. Seb, this is my father, Franklin Fuller."

We shake hands. "It's great to meet you, sir."

"Is it?" Frank keeps hold of my hand, which forces me to stay close and look him in the eyes. "If so, I'd thought you'd have made my acquaintance earlier. Perhaps even asked me for my daughter's hand."

His voice starts out friendly but gets gruffer as he goes along. He raises an accusatory eyebrow at the end, like a nonverbal exclamation mark.

"I . . . I'm sorry, sir—"

I feel like I've been caught releasing a jar full of spiders in the girls' bathroom in elementary school again. I knew Frank would be testy from the way Bea talked about him, but I wasn't expecting a full frontal attack the second I walked into his house.

Bea's mouth opens but nothing comes out for a second. She looks mortified. "Dad, please don't blame Seb. Our engagement wasn't planned. We were in San Francisco last weekend, and the mood struck us. We realized we were meant to be together."

She smiles at me, and I smile back with as much enthusiasm and warmth as I can, even though my hand is going numb from Frank's death grip. Bea's family is watching; we have to sell this.

"Marriage is not a mood, Beatrix," Frank says. "And a gentleman would ask a lady's father for permission before asking for her hand."

"That explains it," I say. "I didn't ask for her hand. I offered her my whole heart instead." I smile, hoping my grand statement came across as sincere and not insubordinate.

"Oh, that's so sweet!" Someone in the family crowd says—a guy with thick, dark hair and a sharp shirt and sweater combo. A trim man next to him with hair the exact same shade as Bea's, except for a few grays at the temple, walks over to us.

"Okay, Dad. You made your point," he says.

Frank finally releases my hand, but he still glowers at me like he might challenge me to a stock portfolio review right here in the kitchen. In my case, it would be a short examination.

The younger man kisses Bea on the cheek and shakes my hand—gently. "I'm Henry, Bea's brother. It's good to meet you, Seb. Forgive us—we're all a little protective of our baby Bea. Come on in and meet the rest of the asylum."

Henry is the sibling Bea is closest to in age, and her favorite. He's married to Rafi, who turns out to be the shirt and sweater combo.

Rafi congratulates us on our engagement, his dark eyes dancing with amusement as he kisses Bea on the cheek, too. "How are you, little sister? Happy to be here?"

Bea widens her eyes at him, like *don't start*. As I make small talk with the couple, I can feel Frank eyeing me. I smile at him, and he turns away.

After a minute, Bea leads me over to three more adults. "This is my brother Thomas, his wife Jane, and Aggie's husband Ben."

"It's lovely to *finally* meet you, Seb." Jane's face is perfectly smooth and glossy, like an over-edited magazine spread. She's as tall as Aggie, but she has long red-blonde hair.

Thomas has dark hair, like Bea and Henry, only it's thinning. He greets me, seeming friendly enough, while Ben looks distracted. Bea told me that both are executives with the Aspen Skiing Company, which runs Aspen Mountain, Snowmass, and two other ski resorts. The whole family lives around Aspen, except Bea.

Bea looks toward the three kids playing with Fluff. "You met Kate already, and that's Will." She points to the boy. He's smaller than his twin, but he has the exact same shade of blond hair. "And my niece Sienna, Thomas and Jane's daughter." Sienna's about five, with curly dark hair and a cute lisp.

The kids are being gentle, but with six overeager hands petting, pulling, and pushing at her, Fluff looks like she might vault over the living room furniture and claw her way through the French doors out to the patio.

"Be careful with her, kiddos," Bea says.

Aggie looks annoyed. "You brought the cat again."

"Dad said I could." Bea sounds defensive.

"Well," Aggie says curtly, "let's have a drink outside."

Bea threads her arm through mine and leans close as we follow Aggie out back. "I'm sorry Dad was so rude."

"It's fine. He cares about you. He wants you to marry a gentleman. I would, too, if you were my daughter." Okay, that sounded weird.

She scoffs. "He only cares about appearances. Like, how dare you not ask him first?"

I didn't ask Bea to marry me at all, much less ask her father for permission, so I don't blame him for being pissed.

The patio, partially covered by a roof, is one of those sweet outdoor kitchens and bar type spaces with screens on two sides that can be lowered with a remote to keep out the cold, rain, or snow. A wall supporting the far end of the patio's roof has a gas fireplace built in. An outdoor television above it has to be great for game days. A long table in the center holds platters of appetizers and at least a case of wine.

Bea pours me a Cab, which we'd already established was my favorite, and we step away from the group to admire the fantastic views. The Roaring Fork River flows through the valley, aided by snowmelts from the peaks above. Bits and pieces of town are visible down below. I point out a hawk floating, wings spread wide, across the pale blue sky. I wish I had my camera.

I pull myself away from the view when Bea's hand grips my arm hard, and her body goes rigid next to mine. I follow her gaze to a well-built redheaded man, about Bea's and my age, sauntering around the side of the house with a grin on his face.

I look at Bea questioningly. I've met all the family she said would be here, but she clearly knows this guy, and she's still clutching me like she's drowning. I hold on to her, worried she's about to pass out.

"What is he doing here?" she asks.

The man shakes Frank's hand like they're old cronies despite the age difference. "Who is that?"

"Reid. My ex."

Chapter Sixteen

❦

Sebastian

Why is Bea's ex-fiancé here? Did she invite him? Judging by her reaction, I don't think so.

Jane spots the newcomer and wraps her arms around him as he reaches the patio. "You made it!"

Reid works his way around the group, hugging and shaking hands like a visiting celebrity. When he gets to Bea, he leans in and kisses her on the cheek. She's still stiff as hardened glue. So am I, for some reason.

"Hey, Beatrix." Reid's voice is gentle. "How are you?"

She doesn't answer, doesn't even meet his eye. She's staring somewhere around the third button down on his dress shirt. The family's watching, while pretending not to.

"You must be Bea's new fiancé." Reid's smile is friendly enough, but his eyes sweep over me like he's appraising a luxury vehicle that isn't quite measuring up. Bea said he didn't start out rich, but his well-cut clothes, leather shoes, and Cartier watch tell me he is now.

And, although I'm not sure why this bugs me, he emphasized the word *new* slightly, like, *you aren't the first explorer to this territory. My flag was planted in Bea's country a long time before yours.*

Well, the joke's on Reid. I have no plans to plant my, er, flag in Bea. In fact, I'm contractually bound not to. Still, when I shake his hand, I can't help squeezing a little harder than absolutely necessary. Shades of Frank.

"How are your cats?" he asks Bea, and then glances at me. "How many does she have now?"

"I'm not sure." It's true, but it doesn't sound quite right. "Enough to make her happy, I guess." I cover Bea's hand on my arm and smile at her. She smiles back, although she still looks shell-shocked.

"Some women collect shoes or bags, Bea collects cats." Reid laughs like it's an inside joke, but Bea's eyes narrow and her lips thin. Henry and Rafi share worried glances.

"What are you doing here?" Bea asks her ex.

Reid looks as if he has no clue she's fuming or maybe doesn't care. I just met the woman, but I can tell she's fantasizing about ways to claw the smile off his face.

"Your father kindly invited me." Reid nods toward Frank. "I hadn't seen the family in a while, and he thought I might like to come for the celebration."

Bea glares at her father, but he's suddenly busy pouring a glass of wine, so she turns back to Reid. "You aren't *part* of this family."

"Beatrix, really." Jane titters nervously, like Bea's joking, although she clearly isn't. "Reid *is* my brother and your brother-in-law."

Reid is family? Why didn't Bea tell me that? The brother of a sister-in-law isn't a close connection, but still, she could have mentioned it. Then again, she didn't mention Reid at all until the drive here. Her eyes are bright with angry tears. Time to step in.

"Hey, Rabbit," I say to her, "why don't we grab another glass of wine and you can show me around the house?"

"Rabbit?" Reid looks at me, then at Bea, his mouth quirking.

"It's a nickname I have for Bea," I say breezily.

This was a little detail I'd planned to surprise Bea with while here. All couples have pet names, right? Bea told me she was named for Beatrix Potter, who created the character Peter Rabbit. And Bea was kind of soft and sweet like a rabbit. I only had a vague idea who Beatrix Potter was until I Googled her, but I thought the nickname was convincing now that I used it.

Except . . . Bea looks horrified. My smile slips.

"Funny," Reid says casually. "Rabbit was my nickname for Bea, too."

I curse to myself. What were the chances the silly nickname I came up with would be the same one her ex used? And why didn't I run it by Bea before I said it in front of everyone?

"Can I talk to you, please?" Bea asks me.

I follow her inside. Her shoulders are tight as she walks a little in front of me. Henry touches her arm as we pass and then studies me with either confusion or suspicion. Maybe both. I can feel everyone's eyes on our backs.

Bea marches through the kitchen, past a grand dining room, and straight into a hall closet. She drags me in and closes the door behind us. Coats, snow boots, and a vacuum crowd the space around us.

"Why did you call me that? How did you even know about Reid's nickname for me?" Her lips quiver, but she keeps her voice low.

"Bea, I *didn't* know," I whisper. "How could I? It was a total coincidence. I thought it would be a nice touch to have something I called you, and I thought of Rabbit after reading up on Beatrix Potter."

"Ugh." Her chin drops to her chest. "What a nightmare."

I touch her arm. "I'm sorry."

She lets out a long breath. "Of course you couldn't have

known. You didn't even know about Reid until today. I should have told you about him earlier, but I had no idea Dad had invited him."

Knowing about Reid would have been helpful, but I understood. He was obviously hard to talk about, so socializing with him had to be torture. It wouldn't be easy to spend time with Sam, my ex, without warning, either, and we mutually decided to end things because of her job offer.

"I'm sorry I freaked out," Bea says again. "I should be angry with my father. I don't know what he was thinking."

"When was the last time you saw Reid?"

I'm interested but also distracted by Bea's citrus and salt scent again. Which makes me want to lick her. Wait, that doesn't sound right . . . but doesn't make it not true, either. Fighting the urge, I lean a little closer.

"I've seen him a couple of times at holidays." She wraps her arms around her body like she's cold. I yank a man's jacket off a hanger behind her and drape it over her thin shoulders. The jacket smells faintly of cologne. "But it was always a big enough group that I didn't need to say much other than hello."

"Was your father happy you were engaged to Reid?" I ask.

"Everyone was okay with it, I guess. Thomas and Jane dated in high school, went to college together, and got married right after graduation, like the perfect fairy-tale relationship. Since Reid and I are the same age, my mom always invited him to come around with Jane. We spent a lot of time together." She fingers the sleeve of the coat.

"If they said Reid was only after your money, didn't anyone think Jane was after Thomas's money, too?"

She raised a sarcastic eyebrow. "She's a woman. *That's* considered normal. But a man needs to make his own way." She mimics her father's voice. "Anyway, Dad was willing to help Reid get started. After Reid got his real estate license, my father helped him with connections to make his first few big sales."

"Then, why did you two split?"

"Reid said he needed time to explore his *options*." She put her fingers in the air like quote marks. "Options. Like I was a country he'd already traveled to, and there were *so* many others to visit." She closes her eyes for a second. When she opens them, they're bright with tears again. "We weren't casually dating; we were engaged. We'd been looking at venues and choosing invitations."

I think about Reid and his flag again, but quickly shake the thought off. "He sounds like a jerk."

She shrugs. "He wasn't always. People change."

So, is she defending him? I can't tell.

"What do you want to do?" I ask. "Are we staying? Confronting your dad? Egging Reid's car?"

She smiles. "I wouldn't waste the eggs. No, we're staying, and we're pretending it doesn't bother us that he's here."

I nod and almost touch her head with my chin. We've somehow moved even closer since we holed up in the closet. I can feel her body heat and smell the chardonnay on her breath, and I have a strong urge to . . . not kiss her. I back up a step and bump into the door.

"How about a tour of the rest of the house?" I ask to save my sanity.

I hang up the jacket I slung over her shoulders, as she peeks out of the closet. The hallway's clear. She takes my hand and leads me to her father's study off a short hallway on the other side of the entryway. It has a huge desk, walls of hardcover books about business, history, and country music. I glance at Bea; so she didn't get her love of country only from her friends after all. The office is also full of animal heads; she told me her dad's a big hunter.

Frank's bedroom is next along this wing of the house. The room is decorated simply in neutral colors. He keeps it neat, but there's no sign of Bea's mother left. Not even a picture. Strange.

Next, we grab our bags, and Bea takes me back past our coat closet to the other hallway with four bedrooms off of it. We end up in a lavender one with posters of Lady Antebellum, Kenny Chesney, and several posters of cats. Has to be Bea's room. The double bed is covered in pillows and plush animals, including— what else? Several stuffed cats. I sit down and jump when a black and white one moves.

"Fluff!" Bea sits beside me and pulls the cat into her arms. "She hides in here when the kids get a little too grabby with her. Aggie and Thomas don't let their kids have pets."

She waves an arm around. "Welcome to my room. Or, I guess I should say our room . . . if that's okay. Aggie assumed we'd be sharing."

Our room. Something slips through my body that I try to pretend isn't desire. "No problem. I can take the floor."

"You take the bed. I'll sleep on the floor."

"Nope. Whatever your father says, I *am* a gentleman, and a gentleman doesn't let his fiancée sleep on the floor. Wait, won't your dad have a problem with this? I thought he was pretty traditional."

"I have three older siblings. Once they were engaged, he gave up on trying to prevent them from staying in the same rooms when they visited." She touches my arm. "I'm so sorry again that Dad said that."

I scratch Fluff. "Seriously, it's okay. And he was right. I should have asked him for your hand. I mean, what was I thinking?" She laughs a little, which is good to hear. "So how do you want me to play it with Reid? Like, should I be buddies with him, jealous, ignore him?"

She kisses Fluff on the head, and a sly smile steals over her face. "I have an idea. But I'm not sure if you'll be okay with it."

I tip my head toward her in a bow. "At your service, miss. What do you require?"

She crosses her legs and taps a sandaled toe up and down. "What if we give my family what they're looking for? Let's act completely, totally, helplessly in love to convince them our fake engagement is for real." She glances at me, the smile still tugging on her lips. "What do you think?"

A vision of posting my camera for sale on Craigslist flashes through my mind, and I shove it away. Not going to happen, no matter how much fun kissing Bea sounds.

"Let's do it."

Chapter Seventeen

❧❧❧

Beatrix

As Seb and I head back to find the family hand in hand, I marvel at how understanding he's being about all this. From my dad's attack to my ex showing up at what's supposed to be a family celebration of our engagement, I wouldn't blame Seb for making a run for it. But instead he stayed, listened, and, he was supportive. And his sandalwood after-shave smelled amazing in that closet.

To top it all off, now Seb has to lay the love act on thick, which I'm sure he'd rather not do. After all, I'm a romance-writing, cat-obsessed freak who has to pay a guy to pretend to want to marry her. Reid didn't want to marry me by the end. And while Seb seems like a good guy, I doubt he'd feel any different after actually dating me.

Seb pulls me aside before we reach the kitchen. "Hey, I should ask before we go in, how far do you want to go with this?"

"What do you mean?"

"I mean physically. If we're going to look crazy in love, then we need to touch each other, but I don't want to do anything you aren't comfortable with."

"Right." I nod, trying to look as serious as he does while suppressing the sparklers waving around in my stomach at the mention of being touched. What can I say? It's been a long time. "How about this: hugging and snuggling are contractually acceptable." It's easier to say if I make it sound official. "But no kissing. Sound okay?"

"Okay." He scratches the back of his neck, looking disappointed. "I have an idea." He whispers it to me. I grin and agree to the plan.

Seb pulls me behind him and tiptoes into the kitchen. I peek out from behind his back. Everyone's still gathered on the patio. We wait by the large island, watching, until we see Aggie pick up an empty platter from the table outside and head toward us.

"She's coming!" I say.

Smoothly, like he's done this loads of times before, Seb pushes me against my father's giant Viking refrigerator, wraps his arms around me, and buries his face in my hair, his lips touching my neck . . . but not quite kissing it. When he moans, I want to laugh—partly from self-consciousness and partly from amusement—but Aggie can probably see my face. So instead, I run my hands across Seb's back, close my eyes, and part my lips, breathing louder than strictly necessary. And I'm shocked by the jolt of yearning that rolls through me. I've missed this.

Aggie's talking to someone, but her words and footsteps falter as she comes closer. "So then Kate says to her teacher —oh!"

I open my eyes slowly, hoping to look appropriately lusty—which isn't hard at this moment—before focusing on my sister. Her face turns pink, and her features pinch with disapproval, as if she found us having sex on the counters. As a bonus, she has Reid in tow with a second empty platter. His knuckles are white against the edges of the plate.

Seb pretends not to have heard them come in. Instead he

moans again, his breath tickling the sensitive skin of my neck and almost sending me into a fit of giggles. I push him back and smooth my rumpled sweater. Seb leans against the fridge and puts his arm around my shoulder.

"Sorry, Ag, we were, er, enjoying the saffron oysters you made," I say.

"Aphrodisiacs." Seb winks at Reid, who looks like he gagged on an oyster himself.

"Reid wouldn't know, he's allergic to shellfish," I say.

"And you're vegan." Aggie's eyes narrow, and her voice sounds suspicious. "Beatrix, can you help me refill these platters, please? Reid, maybe you could refresh Sebastian's drink."

Seb lets me go, but his eyes linger on mine. Did he feel anything like the jolt that ran through me when he was moaning against my neck? He turns away and thumps Reid on the back as if he'd like nothing more than to spend quality time with my ex.

"That sounds great. Thanks, Reid."

With a face as red as hot sauce, Reid leads Seb outside. Aggie stares me down as I pull out wrapped dishes from the fridge.

"What was that about?" she asks.

"Seb and I have a very . . . physical . . . relationship." I want to giggle again at the irony. Our relationship is anything *but* physical.

"You know Dad doesn't like public displays of affection in his home."

Dad doesn't like a lot of things. What's new? I start placing canapés on the platter. "It's our home still, too, Aggie. Mom didn't have anything against showing love and affection."

Aggie eyes the fridge as if we left smudge marks. I wish we had.

"*That* was more than affection," she says.

I shrug casually. "We're in love."

She leans a hip against the island. "So you really are engaged again."

74

I narrow my eyes. "Of course I am. Why wouldn't you believe me?"

"Come on, Beatrix, don't be dense. None of us met him before today. Dad's worried. Who is this man? What does he do for a living? What if he's not right for you?"

Not right for me. Code for being with me for my money. A warning I've heard from Dad since I was old enough to date. And something that happens to be true this time.

"He's a bartender and a very talented photographer."

I saw some of Seb's work at his apartment, and I checked out his website. His photographs are beautiful and inspiring.

"What *kind* of photography?" Aggie's eyes slip to the fridge again.

I snort with laughter. "You should ask to see his portfolio. He takes lovely photos of big, round beautiful—"

I was about to say mountains, but Aggie puts her hands over her ears. "I don't want to hear about it."

She loads her platter with fresh cut vegetables and slices a wedge of cheese. With a big smile, I pop a cracker into my mouth. Pretending to make out with Seb—in front of Reid and Aggie no less—made me feel better than I have in a long time. Maybe we could pretend again soon.

"The twins look like they're feeling better," I say through my mouthful.

The kids are out back playing the hook and ring game Thomas put up for them last year. It's deceptively hard to swing the weighted ring that hangs from the patio roof onto a hook screwed into the wall. Sierra looks red in the face, like she's working up to a good cry. She probably isn't getting as many turns as her older cousins, as usual. Ben stands apart from the group, talking on his cell phone.

"Yes, they are." Aggie's eyes are on the kids.

"How's Ben?" I ask.

My sister's gaze locks on her husband. "He's perfectly fine. Why?"

I blink at her sharp tone. "It's only a question, Aggie. I didn't get to talk to him when I came in."

"He's busy with work."

Her voice indicates that's the end of the story. I didn't even know there was a story.

"Okay. Sorry I asked."

Aggie's shoulders droop, but she doesn't say anything else. I want to ask her if anything's wrong, but I know she won't tell me if there is, and anyway, I can't seem to find the words. She tilts her head at the other loaded platter. "Get that."

Yes, ma'am.

We walk outside, where Dad holds court with one arm around Thomas and the other around Reid. Seb stands nearby, listening.

"Beatrix." My father's voice is too loud, like he's a few glasses of wine ahead of the rest of us. "I was telling Sebastian about our plans."

My pulse picks up. What plans? No one told me about any plans.

"The boys and I are going hunting the next two days, and I've invited Sebastian to come along."

My stomach flops like a dying fish. "Hunting? In June?"

"After the mild winter, the whitetail populations need culling. I got special licenses. We'll stay at the cabin."

Seb's eyebrows furrow with confusion. *Cabin?* I don't think I told him that Dad has another piece of land and a hunting cabin a half-hour away, deeper in the mountains.

Reid claps my father on the back. "Sounds great, Frank."

"I'm in, Dad," Thomas says. Ben agrees, too, although neither looks all that happy about it.

Seb smiles. "Thanks for the invitation, Frank, but I don't hunt."

Henry speaks up. "That's all right, Seb. Rafi and I don't hunt either. Neither do Jane, Aggie, and of course not our Bea."

Dad grips Seb's shoulder. "Yes, it's no problem, Sebastian. You can stay with the ladies."

Henry stiffens, but Rafi touches his arm with a warning look.

"Actually, if it's okay, I'd love to go and do some shooting," Seb says. Dad looks confused, so Seb adds, "With my camera."

"Artsy type, are you?" Dad sounds friendly, but his blue eyes flick up and down Seb like he might as well be wearing a skirt.

"That's me." Seb smiles again, and I admire how natural it looks. I want to pour sand down Dad's pants for being so rude.

"Well, there's plenty of gorgeous scenery for you to photograph around the cabin. The mountain property is stunning." Jane beams at Dad. She's always kissing his butt.

"I have to go," Ben says abruptly. His eyes find Aggie's. "An appointment came up."

My sister's lips thin. I can tell she wants to argue with him, but she won't in front of everyone. Ben makes quick work of his goodbyes, including shaking Seb's hand and hugging the twins. He kisses me on the cheek.

"Congratulations, Bea. Happy for you." But there's something in my brother-in-law's eyes that I don't like, something guarded that wasn't there the last time I saw him. And then it's gone and he's gone, so I can't even be sure I saw it.

I move over to Aggie, who's corralling dirty dishes at the table.

"Here, let me help," I say.

"I've got it."

I hesitate, sigh, and head to Henry and Rafi instead.

Henry nudges me. "Seb seems like a nice guy."

"And he's yummy." Rafi winks at me.

Henry blinks at his husband. "Yummy like the fish with white asparagus in Tokyo? Or yummy like Jamaican jerk duck breast with black jollof rice in Atlanta?"

"Oh, don't talk dirty to me like that." Rafi kisses Henry. "Yummy like . . . lobster mac and cheese on a cold night in Maine."

"When have you ever been to Maine?" Henry asks.

"Years ago with Luc." Rafi waves a hand around.

My brother rolls his eyes. "Luc. Ugh. You only dated him because you had an unhealthy thing for Luke Skywalker."

Rafi nods at me. "It's true."

"Anyway, Bea," Henry lowers his voice, "why didn't you tell me your relationship had gotten so serious?" He sounds hurt. "You barely talked about having a boyfriend. And I could have sworn you told me his name was Jeremy when I visited you last year and he was out of town."

I hate lying to them, but Rafi can't always be counted on to keep secrets. And Henry can't be counted on not to share everything with his spouse. So—I lie.

"He's always been Sebastian."

"Well you look awfully happy together," Henry says.

I blink. We do?

"And he can't keep his eyes off of you." Rafi tilts his head toward Seb.

I follow his gaze and catch Seb looking at me. His eyes move back to Thomas quickly and he nods as if he was paying attention all along. I bite down on the smile that jumps to my lips.

"He's not the only one, either," Rafi says. This time he widens his eyes at Reid. I make a face. I have no idea what motivated my ex to show up today, and I won't bother to wonder.

"Is Seb okay with Reid being here?" Rafi asks.

"Are *you* okay with him being here?" Henry looks worried. Memories of months of sobbing phone calls after Reid and I broke up are probably replaying in his head.

I think about it. "I mean, I wonder what Dad's up to by inviting him, but I'm surprisingly okay."

Not long ago, seeing Reid unexpectedly would have equated to having a hot poker jabbed in my heart. Today was a shock, but even after Seb's tactical error with my nickname, the feeling faded quickly. Now, I only register a dull ache in the general vicinity of my chest.

Am I over Reid? Or is having Seb here making a difference? As if he can hear my thoughts, Seb meets my eyes and smiles. Henry doesn't miss it.

"I'm so happy for you, baby Bea. You deserve someone who loves everything about you, like Rafi and I do." He kisses the top of my head and then tickles my ribs, making me squeal and spill my drink. Ugh, brothers.

I relax a little. If I can convince Henry and Rafi that this engagement is real, then that's one quarter of the war won.

Except, winning the war will result in Seb and I breaking up. I touch my stomach.

Funny how those oysters I didn't eat could make me so queasy.

Chapter Eighteen

Sebastian

I sit on the bed with Fluff as Bea says the last goodbyes to her family. Everyone except Frank is heading off to his or her various homes around town. A few minutes later, Bea comes in and closes the door to her room. She puts her back against it and drops her chin to her chest for a second. When she looks up, she's smiling.

"Seb," she whispers, "you were *amazing*." She sits beside me, leans against the pillows, and draws up her knees. "Everyone loved you."

I raise a skeptical eyebrow. "Your dad? Aggie?"

She waves a hand. "They'll take more time. But Thomas, Jane, Henry, and Rafi all seemed sold on you."

I lay my head back against the pillows, too, but continue to scratch Fluff. I'd learned that if I stopped, I'd have either scratches or a gentle bite to remind me that nothing could be as important as tending to her needs.

I asked something I'd been wondering about since I met

Frank. "Was your father okay with Henry being gay?" Somehow I didn't think he would be.

"Ha, no. When he came out in college, Dad threatened to disown him. It took a few years of Mom and I working on Dad before he accepted the fact that one of his precious progeny dared to be born gay. I think Dad assumed Henry would keep everything private, so when Henry announced he was marrying Rafael a few years ago, he blew a fuse again and almost didn't attend the ceremony." Bea shakes her head and scoffs. "Not only is Rafi a man, he's Latino."

"Shockingly bad manners of him to be both," I say in a snooty voice.

Bea laughs. "Right? Anyway, we aren't sure what changed Dad's mind, but he showed up at the last minute and actually behaved. Mom was gone by then, and I hated that Henry wouldn't have a parent there, even if it had to be Dad."

I wish she'd tell me what happened to her mom, but she doesn't, so I don't ask.

"I wouldn't blame Henry and Rafi a bit if they didn't have anything to do with Dad, but luckily for me, Rafi has a thick skin, an excellent sense of humor, and he values family. He talks Henry into at least coming for holidays and big family events. Although half the time they end up leaving early with Henry angry at something Dad said."

"They're good guys," I say. "I'm glad they're here." I yawn.

"Tired?"

I nod. Today was harder than I thought it would be. I worried constantly about making another mistake like I did with the nickname thing. And frankly, I'm a pretty honest guy. Lying is exhausting.

Bea touches my arm. "Thank you again. I know my family isn't easy to deal with."

I close my eyes and lay the non-cat-scratching hand on hers. "You're welcome. And they weren't that bad. A little . . . uptight, maybe." *Pretentious* came to mind first, but I'm not sure how she'd take hearing that. I pop an eye open to judge her reaction.

"Uptight—that's one way to put it." Bea takes off her glasses, rubs her eyes, and doesn't put them back on.

I haven't seen her without glasses before. Her mismatched eyes are ridiculously cool. I've thought she was pretty since the second I plucked her off Walnut Street, but she's somehow even more beautiful now, even after a long day of family togetherness.

My eyes stray to her mouth . . . and I drag them up again. We'd taken every chance to touch while around her family—holding hands, arms around each other, even nuzzling once or twice—but now that we're alone, that's all off limits. This arrangement makes perfect sense to my brain, but my body is confused.

Bea's cell phone rings. She frowns at the screen before answering it.

"Hey Travis, is everything okay?" She listens. "Okay. I'm up in Aspen this week, but I'll let Gail know where to pick up the medication." She listens again. "I'll tell her. Thanks so much for calling. Say hi to Amelia for me." She disconnects.

"Your vet?" I guess. "He works late."

Since I have Fluff, Bea pulls a stuffed cat into her lap. "Travis is fantastic. He owns the Love & Pets mobile animal clinic."

"Is one of your cats sick?" I ask.

"My new foster kitten. My poor cat sitter had to send Travis a urine sample."

"How exactly do you get a urine sample from a cat?" I eye Fluff, picturing trying to hold a cup under her while she pees.

"You don't want to know." She yawns and stretches her arms above her head.

"Time for bed?" I ask.

As soon as I say it, I'm acutely aware that I sounded flirty. We're sitting inches apart, close enough that Bea touches me almost every time she moves. And every time she touches me, I want her to touch me again. I think for a second that she might be leaning closer, and my whole body tenses with anticipation. But she's only sliding her legs off the other side of the bed to stand.

"Okay if I use the bathroom first?" she asks.

She pulls some things out of her suitcase and heads for the attached bathroom, closing the door behind her. I lay on the bed waiting for my turn, willing my heart rate—and other body parts—to settle down. I usually sleep in my boxers, but I think a t-shirt is in order for this sleepover. If not a full suit of armor.

Bea comes out with her hair in a messy bun, her face pink from scrubbing, and wearing pajamas with cats on them. What else? The slim tank top and short shorts perfectly show off her shoulders and legs. I fight to keep my eyes anywhere but her. I'm fighting so hard, I don't realize she's spread a blanket on the ground next to the bed and is about to lie down on it.

I jump to my feet, startling Fluff, who shoots off the bed and under a chair in the corner. "No way. That's my spot."

"Seb, I've already dragged you away from your life and allowed my family to insult you multiple times. Please, at least take the bed."

"Not doing it. My reputation as a gentleman is at stake here. What if there's a fire, and your father comes to warn us, and he sees me all curled up in your bed while you're on the floor? This marriage will never happen."

"It's never happening anyway. Take the bed."

I shake my head. "I'm going in that bathroom to brush my teeth, and when I come out, if you aren't in this bed, I'll carry you there."

I'm joking, but the vision of carrying her to bed makes my body burn hot. Bea's face looks pinker, too.

"So, anyway, take the bed." I grab my toiletry kit and a t-shirt from my bag and retreat with as much dignity as I can. Except the mirror tells me my hair's a mess and my shirt is stained. So much for making a good impression.

I set my stuff down and plant my hands on the counter,

staring at my reflection. When I first met Bea, I figured this would be a simple job. Spend some time together, pretend to be engaged, split up. Easy peasy.

But the more time I spend with her, the harder this is getting. Being engaged, while far-fetched, doesn't sound ludicrous anymore. And breakups still suck.

I run my fingers through my hair, making it worse. This is a paid job. A job that requires me to sleep a few feet away from a sweet, smart, and sexy woman, yes, but still a job. Pull yourself together, Seb.

When I go back out, the room is dark except for the glow of the bedside table lamp. Bea's in the bed, her eyes closed. At least I don't have to follow through on my threat to carry her there . . . except imagining doing it makes my, er, flag wave. Crap.

I lie down on the blankets. While I was in the bathroom, Bea must have laid out a thick fluffy comforter on the ground, followed by a sheet and a quilt that she laid back for me. One of her pillows lies at the top.

I reach to turn off the table lamp, while Bea does the same. Our fingers touch.

Without thinking, I take her soft, warm hand in mine, caress her palm with my thumb, and intertwine our fingers.

She doesn't say anything . . . and she doesn't pull away. Her breath hitches in a way that makes the rest of me stiffen. After a few minutes, I let her hand go, roll over, and resign myself to getting no sleep whatsoever.

Yeah, this job won't be hard. Not at all.

Chapter Nineteen

✿

Beatrix

The next morning is a flurry of getting the hunters ready to go. Dad, always the Supreme Commander, gives orders, but only Seb pays much attention to what he's saying. Thomas, Ben, and Reid seem more interested in packing the Yeti cooler with beer for the next two days.

My brothers don't enjoy hunting; they're humoring my dad. Reid actively dislikes it, or used to, but you'd never know from the grin on his face as he jokes with Thomas and Ben.

Aggie, Jane, and I are on the couch with hot drinks. Fluff is in a chair, stalking the tassel of a throw pillow.

Jane studies her fingernails. "I need a manicure before the party. Any interest in meeting me at the spa later, you two?"

"Thanks, but I have to get some writing done." I'd set aside the elusive scene in *The Long Trail to Love* for now, but I'm plotting a new book.

Aggie sighs. "Can't you take a vacation once in a while?"

I don't have the guts to admit that writer's block had forced me to take vacations the last few months. That, plus Aggie's tone, makes my reply snappish. "Not right now. I'm under a deadline."

"Well, I'd love your help with something today, if you have a minute," Aggie says.

I agree, wondering what it is, but she's watching Dad now.

Our father sounds as strong as ever, giving orders of what should go where. But he holds on to the counter, looking frailer and thinner than he did the last time I was at home. Frail was never a word I'd used to describe my father before.

Reid, Thomas, and Ben pour ice into the cooler, and Seb is making roast beef and tomato sandwiches.

"How did you meet Seb again?" Jane asks. "We want details, Bea."

I take a long sip of my tea to buy time. Jane hasn't been interested in my love life since her brother dumped me. So is she asking for herself or for Reid? I can't handle being interrogated at nine in the morning.

"I should go help with the food."

I stand and stroke Fluff. She's captured and subdued one tassel and is targeting a second. Out of the corner of my eye, I catch Aggie and Jane exchanging a look. Are they on to us? I move away in a hurry.

"Hey, can I help?" I ask Seb.

He smiles at me, and time skips a beat. I'm actually glad to have a little distance from him today. All the touching and snuggling yesterday, including holding his hand last night before we fell asleep, was far too comfortable.

Although Dad couldn't know this, his accusation about Seb was unfair and untrue. Seb had been every bit the gentleman from the moment he pulled me out of the path of the speeding Tesla to the way he insisted on sleeping on the floor last night. Well, except for the episode against the fridge. I remember Aggie's face and giggle.

"What?" Seb passes me the bread and meat.

"Oh, just remembering the fridge." I slick mayo on the bread.

He nudges me. "Oysters never tasted so good."

I smirk. I'll bet seeing us like that curled Aggie's oysters. My sister was even more disapproving than usual last night. Maybe it was Seb and my antics, or . . . maybe it has something to do with Ben.

I glance at her husband. Thomas and Reid are laughing about something, but Ben looks like he's miles away. As my longest-standing brother-in-law, I know him best of all my siblings' spouses and partners. Usually, he's jovial and jokey, the life of the party.

I wish I could talk to Aggie about it, find out if there's something I can do to help. I wish that was the kind of relationship we had.

"You don't have to go if you don't want to," I say.

He smiles at me. "It gives me the chance to shoot."

My shoulders relax. "You're pretty easy to have around, did you know that?"

He expertly halves and wraps the sandwiches. "Check with my mom before you decide that."

I shake my head. "I can't imagine you were a handful."

His eyebrows rise suggestively. "Actually, I can be two handfuls when I want to be."

He's joking, but my gaze still slides down his flannel clad chest and flat stomach, stopping shy of the zipper of his jeans. My eyes snap back to his, which look hungry for something other than roast beef. Wait . . . what are we doing? I step away.

"Have a good time. Hope you get some great shots." I wipe the crumbs off my hands and head back to the relative safety of Fluff.

Distance. Definitely, distance.

Aggie, Jane, and I wave as the guys take off in Dad's truck. Ben's driving, Dad's in the passenger seat, and Seb is squashed between Thomas and Reid in the back. Our eyes meet, and I mentally wish him luck.

"Well, ladies, I'm off to run some errands," Jane says. "Let me know if you change your mind on the manicure, Beatrix." She slides into her navy BMW and disappears down the driveway.

The kids are in the game room downstairs. Dad has everything from a small bouncy house to a miniature roller coaster for them to play with and on during the long, snowy winters in Aspen. He also has a movie room with dozens of Disney movies on repeat. Soon, I hope, the twins will want to ski, snowboard, snowshoe, or hang out with their friends, but for now, they enjoy messing around with their cousin in the mini-carnival that is Dad's basement. Aggie and I will keep an ear out for fighting or tears, but we should have at least half an hour of peace and quiet.

"What now?" I ask her. I'd love to get on with my initial plan to write and then go for a solo hike, but I told her I'd help with whatever it was she needed.

"This way. I'll show you what I've been working on." Aggie takes me into a back room in the basement. I think Dad uses the room for storage, but when Mom was alive, it was her crafting room. I haven't been in here in years.

The door's closed, it's dark inside, and the shades are drawn. We tiptoe in as if it's a holy place. After Mom's death, Dad acted like anything having to do with her should be stored away, shut off, and never mentioned. It was his way of dealing with his grief, but it wasn't exactly helpful for processing losing the most important woman in my universe.

I open the curtains and shades to let the sun in. A day bed sits, neatly made, against one wall. The long table Mom used for scrapbooking, sewing, and other crafts is clear and dust-free. Labeled boxes sit against the wall.

I'm surprised. The room looks organized and cared for. Dad's long-time house cleaner, Donna, is thorough, but I doubt she does more than a quick wipe down and vacuum in here most weeks.

Aggie sits cross-legged in front of one the boxes.

"What are we doing?" I ask as I settle beside her.

"Wrapping Dad's gifts." She pulls a pile of eight sleek hard-cover photo books out of the box and hands me one.

I open the book to see a sweet picture of Grandma Fuller holding Dad as a baby. His grin is toothless and his blue eyes twinkle, even in black and white. The next page is Dad as a toddler with his sister, Felicia, and his brother, Robert.

Aggie opens another book, running her fingers across the page. "I scanned all the old family photos, took pictures of scrapbook items, and had them made into a series of matching photo books as a surprise for Dad's birthday. Each book represents a decade of his life."

"Aggie, this is amazing." I look around at all the boxes. There are tons, probably stuffed full of old photo albums and scrapbooks.

I open another book, careful not to break the spine. The page I turn to holds a photograph of my siblings and me. It's Christmas morning, and we're sprawled around a massive tree decked out with lights, ornaments, and my favorite decoration, real candy canes. Angels and nutcrackers are displayed around the family room, and snow covers the ground outside the windows.

Mom never held back at Christmas. And she didn't hire a professional decorator, like a lot of our parents' friends did. She did the decorating herself year after year. Or with our help when we could be persuaded to tear ourselves away from school, friends, jobs, and general teenaged laziness.

I remember this Christmas well. I'm about six, so Henry must be ten, Thomas thirteen, and Aggie sixteen. Dad had been traveling a lot and Aggie and Thomas were distracted with their lives, so Henry, Mom, and I did the bulk of the decorating. I felt like a Christmas elf helping Mom string the lights, unwrap each ornament from the storage boxes, and place the star on the top of the tree. It took us two days, mostly because Henry and I had the attention spans of Christmas gnats.

A few days before Christmas, the day Dad was due to arrive home from wherever he was, Mom made homemade eggnog, I helped her decorate sugar cookies, and Henry agonized over the selection of holiday songs to play on the home stereo. We persuaded Aggie and Thomas to be there, and we all waited for Dad to get home, watching a Christmas movie on TV to pass the time.

When Dad did finally arrive, late, we stood with Mom to welcome him in with our hugs, nog, and cookies. Instead, he swept in smelling like alcohol, put his briefcase down, distract-edly kissed Mom on the cheek, patted us on the heads like dogs, and went to bed.

I'll never forget Mom's expression at the moment he left the room: a swirl of anger, frustration, disappointment, and sadness. But the moment she saw us watching, her face changed to a sly smile.

"More for us!" she whispered. "Who wants cookies?"

I touch the Christmas morning photo. My childish face is bedecked with bed-head and shining with joy over my gifts. Mom sits in her bathrobe, smiling and watching Henry and me open and play with our toys, and likely listening to Thomas complain that the gadget he got wasn't exactly right. Aggie sits at Dad's feet, trying to show him a gift. He's reading the paper.

I look at my sister now as she spreads out silver and white wrapping paper. She places the first two books on it and measures before cutting, then hands the roll to me to measure for the next two.

What a labor of love this gift must have been. Mom would have adored Aggie's gift, but Dad? He shoved all these memories into this room and closed the door. Unease passes through me.

I show her the picture. "Remember this Christmas?"

She studies it. "Your hair was always such a mess, Beatrix. And you wouldn't let Mother brush it."

I pull on a lock of my hair self-consciously. I hated the feeling of the brush sliding through tangles when I was girl. And my hair was *always* tangled from running around outside, dancing and twirling, and playing with my one and only cat at the time, Delilah. I sigh and get to measuring.

"He'll love my gift. I know he will," Aggie says in a low voice. She sounds uncertain.

I touch her hand. "Of course he will."

And I really, really hope we're right.

Chapter Twenty

Sebastian

The hunting cabin is a forty-five minute drive from the house through some beautiful country. The views of the valley and surrounding peaks are phenomenal.

Frank's home away from home is about a third of the size of the main house, which means, still damn big. It sits nestled in the forest west of Aspen with hiking, or maybe hunting, trails heading uphill above it. Thomas, Ben, Reid, and I unload supplies and get everything inside.

I figured out from the conversation on the drive up that Frank is too old for the sometimes frigid temperatures, long distance walking, crouching, and occasional climbing that the hunting trips required. So he hung out in the cabin, caught up on the news, and drank coffee and then Scotch while the "boys" crept through the woods freezing their butts off. At least it's not cold in July.

"I can stick around and keep you company," I offer to Frank while the others gear up to go out. I'm actually looking forward to shooting, but I thought he might welcome the chance to get to know me a bit, given I'm supposed to be marrying his youngest daughter. He stares at me like I've suddenly changed into a dress.

"Afraid of a little hiking?"

He's joking, but I have a hard time not rolling my eyes. I've hiked in much harsher conditions than this.

"No thanks, Sebastian," Frank says. "Go enjoy yourself with your . . . camera."

You bet I will, I don't say. I zip up my waterproof jacket, grab my camera bag, and follow the others into the thick forest surrounding the cabin.

"Thomas and I usually go together," Ben says, "so Seb, you're with Reid."

Reid smiles like he won the lottery. I'd rather go by myself but whatever.

Thomas looks at his watch. "We'll meet back at the cabin in a couple of hours for lunch with Dad, then head out again this afternoon. See you guys then." Reid and I walk one direction, and Ben and Thomas another.

I lift my camera. "Hope you don't mind if I wander around. I'll be looking for different kinds of shots than you."

"No problem," Reid says.

"How long have you been hunting?" I ask to make small talk. We can't exactly spend the next three hours in silence. Then again, it's hunting. Being quiet is probably part of the deal. That and drinking beer, given the sheer number of six-packs they put in that cooler.

"Since high school. Frank always invited me to go along when he took Thomas, Henry, and then Ben. He used to say, 'Any son of mine will know how to put food on the table when push comes to shove.'" He imitates Frank's deep, scratchy voice perfectly. "I was seventeen. Didn't exactly have marriage on the brain yet. Sex, yes, but not marriage."

Okay, I *definitely* don't want to hear about the sex he wanted to have with Bea. I change the subject in a hurry. "Henry hunted?"

"He went a few times, but he perfected the art of disappearing in the woods and never actually shooting anything." He laughs.

We both scan the woods as we hike up a narrow trail through the forest. I estimate we're a little below the tree line. I'd love to get above it, but it will be a little while longer.

"So, Bea says you're in real estate?" I ask.

"That's right. Frank got me started there, too. He's an amazing guy in many ways. Accomplished."

Accomplished, and kind of a prick, but again, I hold my tongue.

"How about you, Seb? What do you do?" Reid asks.

"I tend bar. And I'm a photographer. I'm working on doing a little less tending and a little more shooting. Building creative income streams takes time."

Reid shifts his rifle from one hand to the other. "I'm not surprised Bea ended up with an artist."

"Why?"

He grins. "She always loved the tortured artistic types in movies and books."

"I'm not all that tortured, but yeah, since we're both creatives, we understand that passion and frustration pretty well." In more ways than one now that I think about it. Bea had talked about having writers block recently and that her income had dipped because of it. I'd complained about how hard it is to make any money in photography and how long it takes to build a portfolio and a reputation. We understood each other's struggles perfectly.

"I guess it helps you empathize when she has those bouts of anxiety and depression."

Understandably, Bea didn't give me a run down of her mental health history, and it didn't feel right to gossip about it with Reid. But I am curious.

"Her Mom dying was a blow," I say cautiously.

He nods. "They were close. And it was so sudden."

I decide it's safest to agree with him. "Yeah. She said it tore her up that her mom went so fast."

Reid eyes me like a deer in his gun's sight. "Anne had cancer for two years before she died."

I swear to myself and consider grabbing Reid's rifle and smacking him with it. "At the end though. When she died. It was fast."

"Not really. She was in hospice, and the family was all there. Even me."

I clench my jaw. "I'm sure that was comforting for Bea."

Reid walks a little farther. "She hasn't told you much about herself, has she?"

Time to bail out of this conversation before I bury myself any deeper.

"She doesn't like to talk about this stuff." At least I know that's true. Thankfully the tree line is ahead. "I'm going to hike up higher and see if I can get some views of the valley."

"Sounds good. But keep that bright jacket on. Wouldn't want to shoot you accidentally. I'm sure Bea would never forgive me." He winks.

I stalk off, muttering curses the whole way. Great job, Seb. Convincing performance.

❧

During lunch, Thomas, Ben, Reid, and Frank all drink beer and pepper me with tales of the shots taken and missed, close calls, and animals bagged together. After lunch, we switch partners. I'm paired with Ben this time.

He's a lot quieter than Reid—which doesn't bother me. Since he doesn't seem like the chatty type, I decide to stick with him instead of ranging off on my own to find good spots for shooting.

Also, my legs are tired from the steep hiking I did this morning to get away from Reid and his questions.

"This is a good spot," Ben says.

We're in a stand of trees with a small bubbling stream in front of us. Perfect for watching for wildlife. Reid had taken a few shots this morning, and from the lunch chatter, so had Thomas and Ben, but no luck yet in bagging an animal. I got the sense no one was too broken up about it.

Personally, I'd taken plenty of good pictures already, so I didn't mind getting a few of any wildlife visiting the stream and calling it a day. The sun's warm, my belly is full of roast beef, and I'm not with Reid. This is as good as it might get in the next twenty-four hours.

We settle in. After a half hour of silence, with no deer in sight, I decide I ought to at least make a small effort.

"I hear you work for the ski company," I say. "That must come with some nice bennies."

He nods. "You're not wrong. But I'm on the road a lot, too. It gets old."

I can't relate—I've never traveled for work—but I try. "Must be hard to be away from the family. How long have you and Aggie been married?"

"Too long," he mutters. I blink, shocked. He glances at me. "Forget I said that. We've hit a rough patch recently. You've probably already noticed that Agatha and Bea are pretty different."

Um, yeah. Bea's shy, a little odd, and yeah, anxious, but she's also warm and caring and funny once you get past the initial awkwardness. Aggie seems so buttoned up that she's forgotten how to escape the straight jacket.

"Were they always so different?" I ask.

"Not as much before Anne died. The family took it hard." He wipes sweat from under his hatband.

Not this topic again. I won't say a word. Let him do the talking this time.

"Agatha is a lot older than Bea. She and Thomas are close, while Henry and Bea have always been tight. But Anne was always at the center of everything, so when she died, the family sort of . . ." He tents his fingers and then pulls them apart while making an explosive sound.

I nod. My parents and I are pretty close. Dad and I text every day and Mom and I usually talk once a week. Even though we don't live close, they're my rocks. Losing them would be life changing.

"There was before Anne and after Anne," Ben says. "No one was the same."

Families are funny things. Take a picture of one, and you can glimpse the invisible ties that bind—or those that strangle. Take the same shot years later and the bonds may have shifted, but the marks they leave never quite fade away.

"Anyway, I think Agatha tried to step into Anne's shoes, and Bea resented it. Which hurts Aggie." Ben smiles a little at me. "She wants a better relationship with her sister."

"I think Bea wants the same thing." I hope I'm not overstepping, but I'd definitely gotten the sense that Bea wished things were different with Aggie.

"Agatha hopes that after you join the family, Bea might spend more time at home."

The smile freezes on my face. "Yeah, I'm sure she—we —will."

I take a long drink of water to cover my guilt. Being a part of Bea's plan to snow her family seemed okay on paper. But now that I'm here, actively lying to everyone, it's making me more and more uncomfortable.

Frank's an old man. I'm sure that under the bluster he wants the best for Bea. And her siblings are innocent bystanders of the trickery. Even Reid doesn't deserve to be deceived.

I understand Bea's motivation for all this. She wants her inheritance, and her father's belief that she shouldn't get it until she's married seems seriously nineteenth century. Like with full skirts and cravats.

But I can't help wondering: when this fake love story ends will Bea and I be the heroes? Or the villains?

Chapter Twenty-One

Sebastian

That night, I make a fire in the wood fireplace while Ben and Reid cook up the chicken, steak, and potatoes we'd brought with us. To my relief and Frank's irritation, no one killed anything today.

Bea's father sits in a chair in front of the wood fire, holding a glass of single malt that I happened to know was thirteen hundred a bottle. He'd been quietly nursing a series of drinks since we came back this afternoon.

I sit next to him while the others are occupied.

"Everything okay?" I ask.

He glances at me, his eyes a bit bleary, then back to the fire. "Why wouldn't it be?"

I think about leaving it there, but I'm tired of the short answers and challenging questions I'd gotten since I arrived. I guess I've been feeling like I deserve them. But my voice is sharper when I answer.

"I don't know. That's why I'm asking. To see if there's anything you need."

Frank looks like he might throw a dart at my head, but he turns back to the fire. "There's nothing you can do."

Which isn't the same as everything being okay, but the man clearly doesn't want to talk about it with me. I help Reid get the food plated and bring it to the knotty dining table in the corner. This one isn't as grand as the table at the main house, but it fits the cabin well.

"Dinner's ready," Ben says. "Okay if we have a sniff, Frank?" He raises the bottle of Scotch. The older man narrows his eyes, which makes him look like an aging but proud lion. He nods.

We sit down to eat. Reid does his best to entertain with a story about a client who flew in to Aspen from Dubai for one hour, toured a slope-side property, and purchased it on the spot in cash, but Frank's obviously not in the mood for small talk. Ben doesn't say much either, so Thomas, Reid, and I carry on as well as we can.

Reid has started in on a new story when Frank interrupts. "Benjamin."

Ben looks up.

"I got a phone call today. One I hoped never to get."

Ben goes pale but doesn't say anything. The rest of us glance at each other, confused. Actually, Thomas doesn't look quite as lost as Reid and me. He looks wary.

"Agatha has taken very good care of me since Anne died," Frank says.

Ben still doesn't speak. He wipes his mouth and crumples the napkin in his lap.

"And she's taken good care of you. She gave you two beautiful children, and she's managed everything at home so you could succeed in your career."

"I know all that, Frank—"

"Don't interrupt." Frank's blue eyes blaze. "I love my daughters." This time Frank's glower turns from Ben to me. "And I don't want to see them hurt."

"You're one to talk," Ben mutters.

Frank slams down his glass. A less expensive crystal would have shattered. "God knows I've made my mistakes with my family. But I damn well won't sit here and watch other men hurt them if I can help it."

Thomas asks, "Dad, what's this a—"

"Don't act innocent, Thomas. You should have told your sister."

Thomas shoots a look at Ben and then down at the table.

"Take care of this, Ben. Now. Or trust me when I say I'll make sure you don't see another cent of Agatha's money. Do you understand?"

Ben's nostrils flare, and he swallows hard as red patches rise on his cheeks. He opens his mouth as if to argue or explain or something, but in the end, he only nods.

Frank's face softens slightly. "My Aggie may have a cold exterior, but you know as well as I do that her heart burns hot. She doesn't deserve this treatment. So consider this well-meaning advice: come clean and repair your marriage. I'll be watching."

Ben still looks like he's silently wrestling some kind of beast, but in the end, his eyes drop to his plate. "Yes, sir."

Frank turns back to me. "As for you—"

I freeze. Uh oh.

"Beatrix may seem like a strong, independent woman—"

She *is* a strong, independent woman, I think, but it doesn't seem like a good idea to contradict him.

"But she's fragile. She hasn't been the same since my Anne . . . since my wife . . ." Frank's eyes glisten. "She needs a man to pull her out of that head of hers and show her there's more to life than romance books and a million damn cats." He blinks hard. "A man who loves her for herself and doesn't leave at the first bump in the road."

Reid's suddenly studying his plate like it's a hot real estate contract.

Bea does deserve all that. Guilt burns hot through my body.

"I'm going to bed." Frank pushes back from the table and stumbles into his bedroom, leaving the rest of us to sip our Scotch in silence.

Chapter Twenty-Two

Beatrix

Seb texted me a few times over the day and a half that he was gone. He said he was fine, he'd had a good conversation with Thomas, and Reid seemed suspicious of us. Well, I'm suspicious of him. I tried to get something out of Aggie about how he happened to be invited to the house when Dad knew I was bringing Seb, but she only said Dad wanted his family around him for the celebration.

Reid isn't family! I wanted to shout. I mean, technically he's related to Jane and we all spent years together and everything, but he doesn't belong here right now. Of that I'm sure.

The morning of the party, Henry, Rafi, Aggie, and Jane gather at the house for a war meeting. Aggie assigns us various aspects of pulling the details together. Henry and Rafi are in charge of music, drinks, and bartending, Jane is bringing the floral arrangements up to the house after work, and I'm on childcare until the babysitter Aggie hired arrives. I appreciate everything Aggie's done, but her bossiness makes me grit my teeth.

At least I get to spend time with my nieces and nephew. It's a warm day, so I set up the slip and slide in the back yard and appoint myself the judge of their runs. While Kate and Will slide down dozens of times, and fight over who had the highest number of rotations in their slides (it was Kate), Sienna gets a grass burn on her butt on the fourth run and comes to me, her small mouth screwed into a trembling frown. I wrap her up in a towel in my lap and sing to her. Before long, thumb in her mouth, she's asleep.

My phone rings; Travis is calling me back. "Hey Bea, how are things going up there?"

I glance down at Sienna. Her eyes are jerking under her lids. "So far, so good. There have been a few close calls, but no one's called us out yet."

"That's good, I guess?"

I think I know what he means. The longer Seb and I stick to my plan, the worse I feel about it, but it's too late to turn back now. I have to stay focused on the end goal: a new facility for CCR.

"Gail texted that you checked on the kitten this morning?" I say.

His voice gets serious. "Yes, that's what I'm calling about. She's not doing well. I put her on IV fluids and brought her with me to keep an eye on her. Gail said she thought that would be okay with you."

"Yes, of course. But what do you think is wrong? Shouldn't the medications have started working by now?"

"Yeah, they should have. I'm not sure what's going on, which is why I'd like to keep her close. I'll do a few more tests, try to get her hydrated. When are you coming back to the Front Range?"

"Tomorrow."

"Call me then. I'll do the best I can for her, but I'll be honest, Bea. I'm worried."

A fist closes around my heart. I haven't had Ever for long,

and she's a foster, but I care as much about her as any of my fur babies. Maybe if I'd stayed home with her instead of coming up here to hoodwink my family, I could have prevented the illness from getting worse. Gail is very sweet and incredibly kind to mind my cats when I'm away, but she doesn't care about them like I do.

I swallow hard. "Thanks, Travis, I know you'll do your best for her. Please let me know any news."

"Of course. Good luck with things there."

I hear a female voice in the background.

"And Amelia really wants to know how the plan works."

After the slip and slide, I make the kids lunch and they head for the game room to play. Jane arrives with armloads of flower arrangements, which I help her situate around the living, dining, and kitchen areas. While she chatters, I try to control my increasingly frayed nerves.

I hadn't heard from Seb all day. What happened with Reid? Had Dad caught wind of his suspicions? Did Dad treat Seb so horribly that he'd somehow slipped back to Boulder? And would I blame him?

When the babysitter arrives, I go to my room to shower and change. I bought a dress especially for the party, and I'm excited to wear it. I've just finished blow-drying my hair when I hear a knock at my bedroom door. I open it a few inches to find Seb outside. His cheek is smudged with dirt and his hair's a wreck, but my heart dances at the sight of him.

"Hi." I'm wearing a robe, but I suddenly feel shy.

"Hey, I wanted to see if I should use another bathroom to shower—" His eyes drop to my chest. The robe is pooched open a little at the top, showing my bare cleavage. I clutch the sides together, but not before I catch a flash in his eyes that sends shivers to my knees.

I step back, still holding the robe closed. "Come on in. I'm almost done, and I want to hear how it went."

He drops his bags on the floor and starts to flop back on the bed, but he sees Fluff there and rolls to the side at the last second. "Hey, Fluffernutter. How've you been?"

He pets her, and she rubs the top of her head against his hand, purring. I've rarely seen her seek attention with someone the way she has with Seb. Usually, she tolerates people, not takes to them.

"What happened?" I perch on the bed a few feet away. "You look tired."

He rubs his face. "Between Reid trying to catch me out on everything I don't know about you, Ben's moodiness, and your father's lectures, it was a long couple of days."

"What about Thomas?" I ask.

He thinks about it. "Thomas was okay." He smiles at me. "And I got some beautiful shots."

"Thank you for going." I sidle closer and take his hand without thinking. It feels natural to touch him. And it's something a friend might do, right?

After a second, still lying on his back, he lays his hand on my thigh. I stiffen, but I don't move or push it away.

"You're welcome, Bea. And you don't need to apologize for your family. They weren't that bad; I just felt like I had to be both on my best behavior and have a perfect memory. Not exactly easy with the amount of booze flowing up there."

His touch is scrambling my brain. "I, um, I'm sure you did great. And only one more night to go, then you can get rid of the Fullers forever."

He doesn't say anything for a second, then, he pulls his hand away. "Yeah."

I feel instantly colder, and I realize I would give a lot to have his hand back on my leg. Give a lot? How about Fluff?

The idea sends me to my feet. "Go ahead and use the bathroom. I can finish up out here."

He gathers some clothes from the closet and heads into the bathroom. After I hear the shower turn on, I pull my robe off and slide my bra and underwear on. I'm hooking my bra, my back to the bathroom door, when I hear him knock.

"Hey, I forgot my razor in my bag. Can I grab it?"

I scramble for my robe. "Hold on."

But it's too late. He opens the door with only a towel around his waist. I'm temporarily stunned by the sight of his taut abs and smooth chest, until I realize I'm standing there slack jawed and pretty much naked.

Chapter Twenty-Three

Sebastian

Seeing Bea in her bra and underwear makes my eyes pop out of my head, cartoon-character style. And my flag definitely stands at attention, making me glad this towel is extra thick and fluffy. Wow, she's beautiful.

After a few seconds when I honestly have no control over my body, I spin around to put my back to her. Only, I can still see her in the mirror. I can't help continuing to stare, drinking in the sight of her smooth, pale skin, trim waist, and the lacy bra barely covering her breasts. I close my eyes reluctantly.

"I'm sorry, Bea. I thought you said it was okay to come out."

She laughs. First a giggle, then a belly laugh. I'm not sure what to do, so I open one eye. She has her robe on again.

"I'll just grab my razor." I have to slip between her and the bed to reach my bag, and as I move past, I can feel the curves of her body. I desperately want to take her in my arms, lock the door, and kiss her for days.

Keep moving, Seb. I grab the whole bag and escape to the bathroom. As I go, I catch sight of my camera bag on the bed beside Fluff.

As I stare at my flushed face in the mirror for the second time this week, I can't pretend I'm not having feelings for this woman. I actually missed her while I was gone. But I have no idea how *she* feels, and I'm afraid to ask. While I've had a good time being fake engaged to her the past couple of weeks, in reality, I barely know her, and she barely knows me.

Still, I might be willing to give up not only my camera to spend more time with her, but every damn thing I own. That would have to be easier than resisting my feelings for Bea much longer.

Chapter Twenty-Four

Beatrix

I manage to get my dress and jewelry on, my hair and makeup styled, and Fluff fed before Seb finishes in the bathroom. I slip out of my room and go to the kitchen to see what Aggie needs help with. It's not much.

My sister is a floral-smelling whirlwind in a green silk dress that perfectly matches her eyes and a simple, elegant diamond necklace. Her blonde hair shimmers down to her shoulder blades. She's pushing forty, and she's still one of the most beautiful women I know. Until she looks me up and down and opens her mouth.

"Those heels don't look right with that dress. You should have gone with a nude color."

I know my slinky navy wrap dress fits me well, tight in all the right places, and the bracelets and earrings I chose looked great with it in the mirror. I even wore contacts instead of my cat eyes for the occasion. Seb has seen my weird eyes plenty of times now. No sense in hiding them. I hadn't been as sure about the slim, strappy silver heels when I bought them. I guess they were the wrong choice.

Aggie must see the hurt look on my face because her expression softens. "But you look beautiful, Beatrix, and I'm sure Sebastian agrees." She looks over my shoulder and raises her perfectly shaped eyebrows. "Like I said."

I turn and see Seb frozen in the hallway, his eyes on me. I swear his pupils dilate and his jaw clenches as he takes me in. I've written that line before in books, but I've never had a man react that way to me. I fiddle with a bracelet, smile shyly, and take him in right back.

He's wearing slim jeans, a light blue shirt, and a summer weight navy sport coat with a thin, white plaid pattern. I walk over to him, planning to tell him how good he looks. But I'm a coward.

"We match," I say instead.

"Bea," he shakes his head as his eyes dart down my body again, "you're bewitching."

I'm bewitching. Not, I *look* bewitching. Was that a slip of the tongue? Self-conscious responses tumble through my head to my mouth. I manage to stop at thanking him.

"And you smell like salt and limes again. What *is* that?" He leans in close to my neck.

My skin prickles. "My . . . lotion."

He's still an inch away, when Dad walks in, looking dapper in slacks, a sport coat, and a tie. His white hair, which has a tendency to get bushy when left to its own devices, has been neatly combed. I think he even used product to control the waves.

"Happy birthday, Dad." I think of how Mom would have been standing beside him if she were still alive, allowing him to have all of the spotlight, but equally striking in her own quiet way.

He hugs me to him and holds on for a second, a rare display of affection for him. "I'd like to speak with you for a moment, Beatrix."

"Of course," I reply. "I'll be right back, Seb."

Dad nods to Seb without smiling. We walk to his study, where he sits behind the desk and I sit in front of it. Even after all these years, I still feel like a schoolgirl being taken to task by the principal for smoking on school grounds or something. Not that I ever smoked. Nervous, I pluck a carved elephant off his desk to hold.

"I'm afraid I've been too hard on you, Beatrix. Perhaps more so than your brothers and sister."

"That's okay, Dad. It's in the past. And tonight is about celebrating you, not thinking about regrets." Although I'm trying to keep things light, taking the high road, Dad clearly has something on his mind.

"I want to talk to you about Sebastian."

I close my eyes for a second. "Okay."

"Contrary to what you might think, I like the young man—or at least I did—but that's beside the point. How long have you been in a relationship with him?"

"For a while." I'm sure I look as cagey as I sound. "Dad, what's wrong?"

He taps a manila folder sitting in front of him and passes it to me. Inside are a few pages of what looks like printed social media posts from Seb's Instagram. The pictures show Seb and a blonde woman hugging, laughing, and in a few shots, kissing. She's very pretty, and Seb looks happy, which sends an embarrassing jab of jealousy through me.

"Her name is Samantha Wright," Dad says. "The pictures were posted as recently as a few months ago. You didn't know about her?"

Actually, I do. Seb mentioned he'd had a girlfriend that I think he called Sam. They broke up. What now? Do I act shocked? Horrified? Betrayed?

I sigh. "Dad . . . why do you have these?"

"Some things Reid told me made me suspicious."

Reid. That interfering ginger jerk. I'm breathing hard, trying to control the anger pressing on my chest as Dad goes on.

"There was the issue with your nickname. Did you not tell Sebastian that Reid called you that? And Reid said Sebastian didn't know other things he should have if you are so involved as to be engaged. He's worried about you, as am I. Sebastian didn't even make an effort to hide these." He studies my face. "You don't seem surprised."

I finger the elephant's trunk. "Let's leave Seb's pictures out of this for a minute. I have a few questions of my own. Why did you invite Reid here? You knew I was bringing my fiancé."

Dad squirms, something he rarely does. "Well, to be perfectly honest, I wasn't sure you would actually bring anyone."

"Why not? I said I would."

"Beatrix, you told Agatha his name was Seth, Henry his name was Jeremy, and I believe you told me it was Jay. None of us had heard the name Sebastian. And he was nowhere to be found until you turned up here engaged."

Uh oh. My family was paying more attention than I thought.

"I invited Reid because he recently shared with me that he misses you and would like to spend time with you again. I thought you might want to give him another chance." Dad trails off, and for a moment, he looks very old and very tired.

I press my lips together, shame warring with anger and shock. Dad's meddling, and Reid might still care? This week has totally turned me upside down. My father pulls the pictures of Seb back to him.

"I want to make sure you know who you're marrying. And to think about your choices."

There's a knock at the door. Aggie sticks her head in and looks between Dad and me. "Everyone's here."

My father nods and stands. "Beatrix?"

Still reeling, I get to my feet. I need time to process what

Dad told me but I won't get it; the party's starting. If only I felt like celebrating.

Chapter Twenty-Five

❧

Beatrix

Aggie, Dad, and I pass through to the kitchen where Reid's chatting with Seb. My ex watches us closely, but I don't trust myself to look at him. Seb hands Dad a neatly wrapped gift.

"Happy birthday, Frank. You can open it later. It's a picture I took a while ago that I thought you might like. I framed it before coming up to Aspen with Beatrix."

"That was so thoughtful," I tell Seb, forcing myself to look normal. He doesn't need to know that Dad snooped and Reid snitched.

My father takes the gift, grunting a thank you to Seb, whose smile slips. I take Seb's hand and squeeze it as we follow Dad into the living room where the rest of the family waits to greet him. As everyone hugs or shakes hands, I feel Reid's eyes on me again.

My instinct is to hunch and let my hair cover my face. I've felt humiliated ever since he dumped me. But tonight, my hair's all on top of my head, and there's definitely nowhere to hide in this dress.

I can't believe he truly wants a second chance. Does he have some other motivation? Goosebumps prickle over my skin, although the room is warm enough. Without realizing it, I move closer to Seb. Being near him somehow feels like wrapping up in a blanket during a snowstorm.

After wishing my father a happy birthday, Reid approaches me. Seb puts his arm around my waist. I feel every finger through the thin material of my dress. He doesn't let go, even when Reid kisses my cheek.

"Beautiful, as always. Like French countryside waiting to be explored." He winks at Seb. "Remember our trip to Provence, Bea?"

I flush. We'd been newly engaged, in love—I thought—and we couldn't keep our hands off each other. Dad would have been shocked by the number of local landmarks we didn't see that trip, we were so wrapped up in each other. A few months later Reid was off exploring his options.

"The landscapes were stunning, and the food was delicious," I say coolly. "But other than that, I don't remember much about it. Excuse us, Reid, we need to say hello to Henry and Rafi." I tug on Seb's hand, hoping Reid checks out my butt as I go. He might as well get an eyeful of what he gave up.

After a few minutes, Aggie calls everyone to the dinner table. It looks gorgeous, festooned with flowers and bedecked with Mom's best china and crystal. The caterers, who are set up in the butler's pantry off the kitchen, bring in the first course, smoked salmon bisque. The fish was flown in fresh from Alaska, they tell us. Mine is vegan minestrone full of fresh veggies and beans. Delicious.

I'm seated between Seb and Reid. I'm not quite sure how it happened. I was thinking about how nice Seb's manners are as he pulled out my chair for me, and when I finally looked to my other side, Reid was there. His smile is so familiar and charming. He smiled that same smile when he broke my heart.

At least Henry is across from me. We'd long ago mastered the art of interpreting each other's expressions across the dinner table in response to whatever family volcano was erupting that night.

"Sebastian, tell us about your photography."

Oh no. I can see from the glint in my father's eye that he's asking for a particular purpose. He'd had a glass of something on his desk in his study, and he has a new one now. He's getting louder, and his face is reddening. Not good. Seb alluded to the fact that Dad drank a lot while at the cabin, too.

Seb swallows his sip of wine and wipes his mouth. "I focus on nature and wildlife. Colorado is such a fantastic state for it."

Dad grunts. "Photography. Artists never make a good living."

I frown. "Dad, that's ridiculous. Plenty of artists do. And Seb's an excellent photographer. Maybe you should take a look at his work." I turn to Seb. "Dad has several friends who are collectors. Or what about the ski company?" I ask Ben and Thomas. "Don't you buy framed prints of Colorado scenes for the lodges and hotels?"

As I speak, the caterers take our empty soup bowls away and place a leafy green salad in its place.

Seb touches my arm; his expression is stiff. "Thanks, Bea, but they don't need to do that."

"I'd be happy to take a look," Ben says.

"When?" Thomas grins. "You're never at the office."

Aggie raises an eyebrow. "He most certainly is. He's there constantly."

Thomas and Jane exchange a pointed look that I can't quite read, while Dad blusters on. "I never saw the point of collecting art. Waste of money."

"Well Mom loved art," Henry says. "Don't you remember how she'd drag us to every gallery opening in the valley? Oh that's right, Dad, you weren't there."

His voice somehow manages to be both smooth and pointed. I reach out as far as I can with my toe and poke my brother in the leg. He glances at me, and I glare back.

"I remember," Reid says. "I went to a few openings with Bea after we started dating. Anne particularly loved landscapes of the mountains, didn't she?"

"That was one of her favorites." I point to a painting of Maroon Bells on the wall over the buffet. The Bells are a picturesque spot for campers and hikers, not to mention tourists, and few places are more closely associated with Aspen.

Dad's eyes narrow as he glances at the painting. "When will you get a real job, Sebastian? Or are you planning to live off of Beatrix's inheritance?"

We all go silent except Seb, who chokes on his bite of salad.

"That's rude, Dad." My voice is hard. "Seb can support himself as a professional juggler if he likes. And I make a very good living from my work." At least I did until this past year. Henry toes me under the table this time.

"Your work." My father snorts. I can tell he wants to say more, but with a worried glance at me, Aggie puts a hand on his arm.

"Dad, I have something for you. I planned to wait until dessert was served but now is as good a time as any."

She gets up from the table. I want to ask Dad what else he had to say about my work, but I remember the hours Aggie put into her gift, and I bite my tongue. I won't ruin this for her.

My sister hurries back with the photo books that we'd wrapped in beautiful silver paper with a white bow. She tells the caterer to hold off for a moment on the Australian Wagyu sirloin and Maine lobster entree they were about to bring in. They made me a vegetable tart, which I have zero appetite for right now.

Aggie places the first box in front of Dad and sits. He tears the bow and paper off and holds the photo book in his hand. Aggie put the books together chronologically, and this is the last in the series. A picture of our family is on the front, a few years before Mom died. Dad opens the cover, flips through some of the pages. His fingers rest on a smiling picture of Mom that I know dates from right before she was diagnosed. The bittersweet image stabs me in the heart.

Dad slams the book shut. "Photography, art, books. Sentimental garbage." He tosses Aggie's gift onto a side chair.

She freezes, and for a moment, her eyes brighten with tears. Then she slowly sits back, smoothing her napkin in her lap. If I didn't know her so well, I'd assume nothing was wrong. But she's my sister. I know her almost as well as I know myself.

"Aggie worked for months to put those together for you." My voice is icy now.

Henry's face is mottled, and his eyes are angry slits. "I'd like to see the books, Agatha."

"Me, too." Ben turns around to retrieve the book, which is behind him.

"Oh, now you're interested?" Aggie asks.

I bite my lip. Aggie has a terrible habit of turning on other people when she's hurt or upset.

"Yes, I am." Ben's voice is tight but calm.

"You haven't shown the slightest interest in my project since I started it."

"It wasn't ready to see until now."

Something sparks back and forth between them, an emotion I can't quite read.

Jane lifts her glass to her mouth. Her movements are a little loose, and when she speaks, her words slur slightly. "He hasn't been interested in much the last year or two, period."

Thomas glares at his wife. "Stay out of it, Jane."

"Stay out of it, Jane. It's family business, Jane. Well, I'm part of this family, *Thomas*. And Agatha is my sister, too. I think she should know what's been going on."

The table goes quiet. Even the caterers, who have been making some noise plating the dishes up until now, are silent.

"What should I know?" Aggie's eyes jump from person to person. I glance at Henry. He doesn't look quite as confused as I feel.

Dad glowers. "This is not the time, Jane."

"No? When is the time, Frank?"

"The time to know what?" Aggie asks.

"That your husband is having an affair," Jane says.

Chapter Twenty-Six

※❀※

Sebastian

Oh, crap.

The expressions on Bea's family's faces range from shock and horror to guilt and even a little relief. I think only Bea and Aggie didn't already know. I'd wanted to somehow bring it up with Bea myself, but there hadn't been time.

"Jane, you're drunk." Thomas stands. "We're getting Sienna and going home. Dad, Agatha, I apologize." He hustles Jane out of her seat. She stumbles a little in her heels as they head for the basement door where the babysitter is watching the kids.

Aggie stares at the masterful floral centerpiece, as if it holds all the answers. Then she looks at Ben.

"Is this true?"

He licks his lips and nods.

"How long?" she asks.

"A year or so."

"Who?"

His eyes are sad as he answers. "Does it matter?"

Aggie slams a manicured hand down on the table, sending her forgotten salad fork flying. "Yes, it matters."

Henry stands. "Why don't you two come out to the patio where you can have some privacy?"

Ben walks out immediately. Henry leads Aggie out. Rafi and Bea jump to their feet, but Henry shakes his head. "Stay. Enjoy the main course with Dad."

Salvage this wreck of a night, his look says. Rafi sits after a few seconds. Bea hesitates, and then she sits, too. I can tell she wants to go with her sister, but her expression is uncertain, like she doesn't know if Aggie would want her by her side.

It hurts me to see, so I'd bet it's awful for Bea to feel. I put a hand on her back.

"You okay?" I ask quietly. She shakes her head and blots her eyes with her napkin. Reid touches her arm, and for some reason, I want to reach over Bea's chair and karate chop him. I can't help but lump him in with his stupid, insensitive sister. Maybe Aggie needed to be told, but Jane could have picked a million better moments to do it.

Rafi calls to the caterer. "May we have the next course, please?"

Frank takes a long drink. "She might as well know."

"Not like that," Bea says. "That was cruel." She keeps glancing behind us toward the patio. I can hear raised voices.

"Life is cruel." Frank glances at the painting on the wall again, and then the photo book that's still sitting on Ben's empty dinner plate.

Henry comes back, his face pale, and sits beside Rafi. They seem to have an entire silent conversation in a glance—a trick I've always admired but never had a relationship long enough to master. Bea sniffs, and I rub her back again.

The steak and lobster the caterer puts down looks delicious, but I've lost my appetite. As I look around, so has everyone else —except Frank. He tears into the steak like it's his last meal on death row. Bea picks at her tart with her fork.

Reid eats a roasted potato and then clears his throat. "Have any big travel plans, Frank?"

They talk about a fishing trip to Montana that Frank is taking with a few friends in August.

"Can I do anything?" I murmur to Bea.

She shakes her head. "I wish *I* knew what to do."

I nod. I wish I could help, but I'm in over my head here. My family is nothing like the Fullers. We have our disagreements, but they usually involve a quick flame up followed by an apology and a hug or joke or both. We haven't had a big fight in years.

Bea, Henry, Rafi, and I choke down the main course and take a few bites of the elaborate birthday cake, topped with fresh flowers, that the caterers bring out at Henry's direction. As soon as Frank has eaten most of his large slice, Bea stands.

"I'm going to check on Aggie."

Henry and Rafi get up. "We will, too."

Which leaves Reid, Frank, and me. If Frank is concerned about his older daughter, he doesn't show it. He pours Reid and me an after-dinner brandy and takes a few more forkfuls of the side of the devastated cake. I'm not sure how the man stays trim eating and drinking the way he does.

Frank manages to make small talk, which mostly Reid answers. I decide to see if Bea needs anything outside, when Frank says, "Reid, go out back and get the lay of the land."

"Lay of the land?" Reid asks.

"See if anyone's dead or bleeding."

"Umm . . ."

"Get lost, Reid," Frank says.

Reid folds his napkin and stands. He doesn't look offended or even surprised. "Yes, sir."

Once Reid is gone, Frank gestures to me. "I'd like to talk to you, Sebastian. Bring your drink to my study."

I follow him from the table while the caterers tiptoe in to start cleaning up. I wonder for a second what they're thinking after hearing what went down. I don't know what to think myself.

Bea had shown me her father's office before. With its large desk, dark cabinets, and oiled leather furniture, it's most definitely a man cave. And a hunter's haven. The head of an elk hangs on the wall over the doorway, and a moose noggin looms over the desk, antlers and all. I feel watched.

Frank sits under the moose. "I'll get down to it. I don't know how much Beatrix has told you about her history with men, but it isn't particularly good. She's had one serious relationship before you, and that ended with her in a puddle of tears that didn't dry up for months, maybe even years."

Yeah, and you invited the ass who left her that way to your birthday party, I thought.

"I don't want to see that happen to her again," he says. "And I've discovered that maybe you and Bea aren't as close as she's led us to believe."

Oh, snap. Frank watches me coolly, his hands resting on the arms of his swivel chair. Sweat rises on my scalp. I glance around the room, searching for a response, but zilch comes to mind.

"Nothing to say about that, eh? Well, I have my own theory to test out. Sebastian, I'd like to ask you for a number."

"A number, sir?" Something about Bea's father turns me into an eighteen-year-old Army recruit facing his drill sergeant.

"A number that will persuade you to go away."

"Go away?" A recruit who repeats what the drill sergeant says.

"Leave Beatrix alone."

I freeze, the situation finally clarifying in my brain. "Are you saying you'll pay me to leave Bea?"

He leans forward, threads his fingers together, and fixes me with a polar blue stare. "That's exactly what I'm saying."

My mouth opens, but nothing comes out. What kind of a father offers to pay his daughter's fiancé to go away, even if he does suspect something's not quite right between them?

On the other hand, what kind of guy agrees to be paid to pretend to be a woman's fiancé in the first place?

One who needs cash. The analytical side of my brain is already calculating exactly how much I would need to upgrade my camera, take a one year sabbatical from bartending to polish my website, network locally, and get some prints framed and ready to sell. I could work on the photography book I've been wanting to put together, buy the new long-range lens I've been eyeing, maybe do some traveling—

I blink and focus on a picture shoved deep into the corner of a shelf. A younger Bea, and a woman I think is her mom stand on some steps. Anne is dark haired and petite, like Bea. She's laughing, a thin arm slung around her daughter. Anne's looking away at something or someone, clearly amused, but Bea is gazing adoringly up at her mother's face. Bea's heart has been broken more times than anyone's should be.

Guilt pricks me for even thinking of taking Frank's offer. Bea is already paying me a generous sum, and going away is already in our contract. What would it make me to take her dad's money behind her back?

But what if I didn't take it behind her back? What if I told her about the offer and that I'd like to accept it? My arrangement with Bea was a business deal, after all, pure and simple.

Except, in the last few days, it had started not to feel like one anymore. I knew her well enough now to know that accepting her father's payment to go away would hurt her. I'm not sure I can do that.

"I can see you need to think about my offer." Frank's voice is steely, probably because I look guilty as a preacher in a porn shop. After all, I didn't jump up in protest at the first mention of being paid off. The truth is, I do need to think, but not for the reasons he believes.

"I'll give you until tomorrow to tell me a number. How much is a relationship with my daughter worth to you, Sebastian?"

He stands, so I do, too. He cocks his head thoughtfully.

"I'll add a little . . . wrinkle . . . to my offer."

I blink. Isn't his offer wrinkled enough?

"If your relationship with Beatrix is legitimate, then you're not with her for her money. So you won't mind if she doesn't receive her inheritance until I die."

"I'm not sure I understand."

"I'll make it simple. Go away, and not only do you get paid the amount you want, but Beatrix gets her inheritance now. Stay with her, and neither of you get an extra dollar until I die. Which I don't plan to do for some time."

He swallows the last of his brandy. My hand shakes as I do the same. Well, that seals the deal, doesn't it? I go home and get the chance to grow my photography business. Bea can build the cat facility and probably do anything else her heart desires with her inheritance. It's a win-win for both of us. I raise my empty glass to Frank in a mock toast.

"Oh, and one more thing. If you tell my daughter what we discussed tonight, the agreement is off," he says. "I'll expect to hear from you in the morning."

If I take this deal, Bea and I get exactly what we wanted when we met. So why is there an ugly ache in my chest, a riot in my gut, and the fear that I'm giving up something a lot more important in this bargain?

Chapter Twenty-Seven

Beatrix

"Aggie, what can we do?" I ask.

My sister doesn't answer. Henry, Rafi, Aggie, and I sit in Adirondack chairs around a dark fire pit out back. The temperature is mild and stars twinkle merrily overhead, but no one says anything about the weather.

Ben left—after Aggie threw a wine glass that just missed his head. The shards glitter from the other side of the patio.

When Henry, Rafi, and I first came out, Ben was talking to Aggie, his voice quiet but urgent. My sister stood very straight and still, staring through her husband like he wasn't even there. The rest of us had stepped back inside and then hurried out again after we heard the glass shatter. Ben rushed past us, his eyes red and face anguished.

I'd sat Aggie down, offered to bring her water, a blanket, her children—anything to comfort her. But she hasn't even looked at me.

"Aggie, please." I touch her hand. "Talk to us." Nothing. I exchange a helpless glance with my brother.

"Why don't Rafi and I take you and the kids home," Henry suggests gently.

Aggie stands, so we do, too. When she speaks, her voice is robotic. "No. Ben's going home to collect his things. I'll sleep here tonight." She looks at me but doesn't meet my eyes. "Would you please put the kids to bed, Beatrix?"

"Of course." I catch her hand as she passes by. "I'm so sorry, Aggie. Please come and get me tonight if you need anything."

She nods and pulls her hand away. Henry and Rafi kiss Aggie's cheek and say goodnight, and she walks inside. I check my watch. It's not yet nine o'clock. We have the babysitter booked for another couple of hours. The kids can play a while longer, blissfully oblivious to the earthquake that just collapsed their family.

Henry, Rafi, and I fall back into our chairs, silent for a minute.

"Did you two know?" I ask.

They exchange glances, and Henry answers. "No. I would have told Aggie if I knew . . . but we wondered. Ben hasn't been around much recently. At first, we thought it was his travel schedule."

Rafi twists his cuff holder. "I was flying out of Denver to Phoenix one morning, and I ran into Ben waiting for a flight with a woman. I thought she was a colleague."

Henry goes on. "But then we saw him with the same woman at a restaurant here in Aspen. Maybe it was a work dinner, but they seemed . . . close. I should have asked Ben about her." My brother rubs his face.

"I wouldn't have known what to do, either." I put a hand on Henry's arm.

"Agatha will *never* forgive Ben," Rafi says. "She'll make his life hell."

"I'm guessing she already has," Henry says sadly. "Not that

that's any excuse. He should have been honest about how he was feeling. There are plenty of good couples therapists in Aspen."

"They could have gone to Lydia," Rafi adds.

"She's rich enough off us." Henry pecks his husband on the lips.

I lay my head against the chair. "If only Aggie could relax and enjoy herself once in a while."

Rafi laughs. "You're one to talk, Baby Bea. Although, you do seem much happier—and more relaxed—this week than I've seen you in a long time. And I'm chalking it up to a certain small, dark, and handsome man."

Despite Dad and Reid, I *am* happy. Is it Seb? Or is it because the CCR project feels within reach now . . . thanks to Seb?

"Sebastian survived Dad's hunting trip, and Aggie and Ben took the spotlight off him at dinner, at least. I think you two might have made it through the gauntlet," Henry says.

"They survived—together," Rafi adds dramatically. "Reid, on the other hand, seems decidedly dejected. For Reid."

I'd noticed he was less jaunty than usual tonight. Is he that upset that I'm engaged? One side of the French doors opens. I expect to see Seb, but no. Speak of the tall, redheaded devil. Reid sits down in Aggie's empty chair and hands me a big glass of wine.

"How are things in there?" Henry asks.

"Quiet. Frank and Seb are holed up in his study. Aggie blew by me on the way to her room. The caterers almost have things cleaned up. So I thought I'd join you party people out here."

I smile at the joke. A party this was not. But what are Dad and Seb discussing in there? Is my father accusing him of having a girlfriend? Or something else? I don't know how many more accusations and insults Seb will be willing to take.

"It wouldn't be a Fuller celebration without a brawl." Henry sighs.

Reid grins, his white teeth flashing in the dark. "Oh, I know.

I've been around long enough to have learned a thing or two about this family."

He gazes at me. The warmth in his eyes makes my skin tingle. With attraction? Or is it crawling? I'm not sure anymore. What is he up to?

Henry and Rafi stand. "Well, I think we'll call a Lyft and head home."

I glare at my brother. *Don't leave me out here alone with Reid.* He ignores my telepathic distress signal.

They shake Reid's hand and kiss me on the cheek. "If Dad is still sober when you see him, tell him happy birthday and good-night." They walk around the side of the house. Smart—avoid having to actually see Dad on the way out.

I'm not sure whether to escape inside and rescue Seb or sit and chat with Reid. I decide Seb will tell me later what Dad said. My curiosity about Reid wins out.

"Well, that was a good time," I say sarcastically. "Ugh. My family is a wreck."

"Any time I get to see you is a good time." Reid sounds serious. So much for the friendly chat.

I turn in my seat to face him. "What are you doing here, Reid? Dad confirmed he invited you—"

"Didn't believe me?"

"Why should I? I haven't heard from you, and you barely spoke to me when we did see each other. What do you want?"

He grips the arms of his chair. It's his turn to stare at the sky. "Another chance."

I shake my head and flatten my voice. "Really?"

"Really. I screwed up when I broke things off with you, Rabbit. Maybe I did need to slow us down a little, but I shouldn't have given you up."

"So all the options didn't work out?" I say pointedly.

He rubs the back of his neck. "I deserve that and a lot more."

"What changed? Why are you coming back now?"

"If I'm being honest, it was hearing that you're engaged. Jane mentioned you had a boyfriend a while ago but that you didn't seem serious about him. I thought I had more time." Reid takes my hand. "Bea, look at me." Reluctantly, I do. "We were so serious so young. With circumstances being what they were—"

"What circumstances?"

He raises an eyebrow. "I was just starting out. I had no way to support you. Not the way you were used to."

"You know I didn't care about that—"

"I did. And yes, I was afraid to commit. But we're older now. My business is doing well, and I'm ready for more."

"Reid, Seb is my *fiancé*. I know you took Spanish and not French, so I'll explain. It means we're getting married. What part of that sentence don't you understand?"

Reid looks unfazed. "I understand it. I'm not sure I believe it."

I huff out a breath.

"How well does he know you? Or you him? He didn't know I called you Rabbit or how your mom died. And he didn't even know you were vegan; he was trying to feed you oysters! Anyway, your family's worried about you, Bea."

"If they are, they can tell me themselves." I don't mention that Dad already has.

"Look, I know you'll need time to work things out with Seb, but please tell me I might still have a chance."

"Reid, I—"

He touches my lips. "Don't give me an answer now. Think about it, okay? I want you back, Rabbit. And this time I'm ready for all of it. A home, kids. Whatever you want."

My heart trips in my chest, and my body is so tense I'm shaking. Nothing is stopping me from getting back together with Reid, I suddenly realize. Seb's contract ends tomorrow, and I'm going home to my uninspired book and too quiet home.

"What about my cats?" I ask. Reid always tolerated them, but he never seemed to like them much.

"I love your furry friends."

"I have a lot more friends than I used to."

"The more the hairier." He laughs and leans closer, light reflecting in his blue eyes. "It's good to see you smile, Bea. I want to make that happen a lot more often."

The hurricane of confusion inside is so overwhelming that I don't recognize what's coming until Reid's lips are on mine. The kiss isn't long or particularly passionate, but it's warm and familiar. Like slipping into your own sheets after being away.

The French doors open, and Seb comes out. I pull back from Reid, but too late.

"Hey, I— Oh. Sorry." Seb walks straight back inside.

Reid's expression is wide-eyed but somehow smug, like we got caught making out in the janitor's closet in high school again.

My instinct is to run after Seb and apologize, but then I wonder—why? Seb and I aren't dating, and kissing Reid isn't a betrayal. So, why does it *feel* like it is? My head falls in my hands.

"I'm sorry, Bea." Reid doesn't sound sorry.

"Please . . . go home. I'll call you tomorrow."

"Aren't you going back to Boulder?"

"I feel like I should stay in case Aggie needs me."

He makes a face. "Since when has Aggie needed anyone?"

I gasp. Reid is right. Even when Mom died, Aggie didn't fall apart, didn't show how much it hurt. Not to me, and I doubt to Ben. Aggie has never needed anyone, even her husband. Or at least she's never shown it. Everyone wants to feel needed; especially by the person they love.

I stand, almost toppling my wine glass. "I have to go. Night, Reid."

I hurry to Aggie's door. I don't see Seb, and anyway, that conversation will have to wait. My sister needs me, whether she knows it or not. I knock on the door of her old room, a few doors down from mine.

"Aggie?" I ask. "Are you awake?" No answer. "Can I come in?"

I wait and knock a few more times, but she doesn't open. She's either asleep or ignoring me. I try the door; it's locked.

Frustrated, I go to my room to look for Seb. There's no sign of him. I check the study; Dad's dozing at his desk. An empty glass and a picture of Mom are in front of him. Swallowing the ache, I put my arm around him and help him to his feet.

"C'mon, Dad, time for bed."

He wakes with a low groan. He'll probably have a monster hangover tomorrow. I help him get undressed and into his pajamas, trying to avoid looking too hard at his thin, wrinkled body. No matter how old he gets, I still see him as the young and all-powerful father he was in my youth. But as I help him into bed, his shoulders and back bony under my hands, it's hard to pretend that he's not elderly, frail, vulnerable.

And that's when it hits me: he's my father, but he has no power over me anymore.

If Dad gives me the inheritance money, then great—I can help fund the center. If not, I'll find another way. It might take a while, but I can do it. I don't need Dad or his money. But he needs me.

As I smooth the covers over him, he takes my hand in his shaky one. "Thank you, Annie. I love you."

Tears blur my vision as I find the words I want to say to my father on his 80th birthday, whether he deserves them or not.

"I love you, too."

Chapter Twenty-Eight

Beatrix

I wake up early the next morning to find Seb gone from my room. Actually, I don't think he slept here at all. The bedding is still neatly folded on the chair. Maybe it's for the best. I needed time to think last night after paying the babysitter and putting William and Kate to bed.

I get dressed and slip out to the patio. It's a bright and sunny morning, but the air's crisp and cool and the views are spectacular as always. Making a mental note to sweep up the shards of Aggie's wine glass when I get back, I follow a favorite hiking path that leads up above the house.

Since Reid kissed me last night, I've been reeling like a toy top. A while ago I might have run back to him without a second thought, grateful he was giving me another chance. But now things feel . . . different. Some of it might be Seb, but some is me.

I don't want to go back to the pathetic creature that let a breakup derail her life. I feel a little stronger now. Ready for a new adventure. Ready, maybe, for love again. And that's thanks to Seb. His kindness, his interest in me and my life, even though it was bought and paid for, makes me wonder if I have more to offer than I thought. I don't feel so awkward and anxious around him like I do around most people. And he doesn't even seem that bothered by my dysfunctional family. Seb and I get along well, even under these difficult circumstances.

I stop to watch a hawk swooping through the sky, its wings outstretched like it's joyfully embracing the world and all it has to offer. Seb and I saw a hawk, maybe this one, when we first arrived in Aspen. Is it a sign?

Right then, the bird spots something on the ground. It streaks down, talons outstretched until it disappears from view. Some small, furry mammal is about to be breakfast. Okay, maybe not a sign. I start walking again.

Maybe Seb is just a good actor. Is his sweetness, his supportiveness, all part of the performance? Does he even like me, like he seems to? Of course I'll honor our agreement and pay him the rest of what I owe, but until there's no money and no contract involved, there's no way to know how he genuinely feels.

After about forty-five minutes of hiking, I reach an overlook. As I weave through a stand of aspen trees, I almost trip over someone kneeling behind some bushes.

Seb has his camera pointed up the ridge instead of at the view below. He doesn't speak, so I don't either. I wait quietly behind him.

He depresses the shutter on his camera a few times, a series of quick clicks. Then, he stands, but he doesn't smile at me like he usually would.

"Following me?" he asks, and not playfully.

What's wrong with him? Was it the conversation with my father? Or could it be . . . that I kissed Reid?

"This is one of my favorite walks. When I'd had enough of my family, I would come up here and think about how much easier life would be if I were a moose or eagle or something. Basically, I'd think stupid thoughts and feel sorry for myself."

"Doesn't every teen do that?"

"This was last year." I expect him to laugh with me, but he doesn't. I swallow hard, and my face grows hot. "Get any good shots?"

Seb holds up his camera so I can see the viewfinder. He clicks back through some of his pictures. They're wonderful. Using the early morning light to its full advantage, he's captured both the valley and the ridge from interesting angles. He even managed to get a close-up of a bright yellow tanager on a branch.

"I meant what I said last night. You're an incredible photographer," I say. "Sometimes I feel like pictures of nature aren't very original, but your shots make me want to step into the image."

"Thanks." He packs his camera in its bag and stuffs it in his pack.

Should I say something about Reid? Seb couldn't be jealous, could he? I'd feel ridiculous even implying that given our agreement. Maybe *this* is the real Seb—cold and disinterested—and he's finally letting me see it now that the job's almost over.

As we start back down the trail together, I'm more confused than ever.

"Did you see your father this morning?" he asks.

"No, did you? He's probably in bad shape."

He nods. "He drank a lot."

"No, he *drinks* a lot." I leave it at that for now, but my siblings and I need to talk about what to do to help him at least cut back. "Reid said Dad spoke to you alone last night. What—?"

I stop. The house is in view now. Aggie and the twins are prowling around the backyard, calling out, although I can't hear what they're saying. Even Dad is standing outside in his bathrobe, his hair wild.

"This looks like trouble," I say. We rush down the trail. "Aggie? What's wrong?"

"The cat got out." My sister looks exhausted and irritated.

Kate runs to me. "Will left the door open and let Fluff out! She's out here somewhere by herself!" As her brother turns red and tears leak out, Kate wails, "And we can't find her!"

Although fear claws at me, I hug my niece and nephew. "It's okay guys, we'll find her."

Fluff wasn't much of an outside explorer, so I doubt she would go far, but these are the mountains. Predators, like that hawk I saw earlier, are everywhere. Foxes, coyotes, bears, and mountain lions are all willing and able to eat a small cat like Fluff. If something like that got her, we wouldn't even know what happened. She'd just be gone.

Stop, Bea.

I run for the kitchen cabinet where I stashed Fluff's food. Seb's there digging cans out of the bag I brought from home.

"Thank you." My voice shakes a little. Terrible visions of finding Fluff bleeding, or never finding her at all, are storming my brain.

He hands me a can. "Try not to panic, Bea."

We hurry outside with a few extra cans for the twins, Aggie, and my dad. As we all crack them open, I pray Fluff will hear the distinctive sound.

"Fluff," I call, pacing across the yard, "Fluffernutter! Come here, girl."

The twins and Aggie call to her, too. Dad winces, like his head is splitting, but he walks to edge of the yard holding his can.

Ice slides up my spine with every passing second, and I'm trying to hold back tears. I hate crying in front of my father and sister. They always make me feel weak for showing such a vulgar display of emotion. Mom cried all the time. Commercials were infamous for making her sob.

After a few minutes of calling for her, Dad gives up. Aggie works to keep the twins from running off by themselves to find Fluff.

"Why don't you take Dad and the kids inside and Seb and I will keep looking," I say to Aggie.

My family goes inside, and I keep calling, following Seb into the forest. We split up. I search the tops of the trees, hoping she climbed to safety. When a shout comes from my left, I run that way. The shade makes the contours of the ground hard to judge. But the forest opens up and I spot Seb in front of a pile of boulders and a few downed trees. His back is to me, and his posture is stiff.

"Did you find her?" I ask.

"Yes." His voice is strained. He doesn't turn around, but he slowly stretches a palm toward me. "Stay back."

Something beyond Seb rattles. I step to my left to get a better view, as fear wraps tightly around my chest.

Fluff stands between Seb and a coiled rattlesnake. And the snake has Fluff in its sights.

Chapter Twenty-Nine

Beatrix

Fluff glares at the rattlesnake, her hackles up. *This can't be happening.*

"Was she bitten?" I whisper.

"Not yet."

I'm trying very hard not to react. Fluff's never seen a snake before. Clearly, she instinctively knows it's dangerous, but she probably isn't sure how.

"Fluff," I call softly. "Come here, love. Come to me." Staying back, I crouch down and hold out the cat food can to her. She doesn't take her eyes off the snake. And it's not backing down.

Seb wipes sweat from his eyes, and then very, very slowly, he creeps toward Fluff. The snake lifts its head, still rattling.

"Please be careful!" I say.

Seb lunges, grabs Fluff, and jumps back at the same time the snake moves.

The snake strikes so fast I barely see it, but I hear fine. Seb shouts a curse. He scuttles backward, Fluff in hand, and I hurry to his side. Thankfully, the rattler slips away into the pile of rocks behind it. My heart hammers so hard it hurts.

Seb sucks in a breath and grimaces. Two red dots rise on his left forearm, the arm he grabbed Fluff with.

I yank off the bandana I wore as a headband and wrap it tightly between Seb's elbow and the bite. Then, I call Aggie, quickly fill her in, and ask her to call the paramedics. I take Fluff and put an arm around Seb's back.

We move through the woods toward the house as quickly as we can. But I'm acutely aware that every step sends venom through his body.

Fluff mews and bats at my nose. I kiss the top of her head. "Seb, thank you. Thank you so much."

He nods, his face white, and cradles his bitten arm. He's leaning on me, which makes our progress slow. As we finally reach the yard, an unwelcome redhead appears instead of emergency personnel. Great. Facing Reid and our kiss last night is the last thing I need right now.

"What are you doing here?" I ask.

"I came to grab my phone; I left it last night. Aggie told me what happened. Here, let me get him." Reid takes my place supporting Seb. "I'll drive you to the hospital. It will be faster than waiting for the ambulance."

"Thanks," Seb says through clenched teeth.

Clutching Fluff, I follow them. Aggie, Dad, and the twins come outside when they see us. The twins burst into fresh tears.

"Is Fluff hurt?" Kate asks through the tears.

"No, but she had a scare. Will you two take her inside and cuddle with her?" I hand her to Kate. "Be sure to close the door behind you, okay?"

From her grim expression, I can tell that Aggie would love to remind me again that this wouldn't have happened if I hadn't brought Fluff. I focus on helping Reid with Seb.

"My car's right out front," Reid says.

"So is mine. I'll drive him," I say.

"Rabbit—"

"Don't call me that."

"Bea, let me drive. Ride in the back with him in case he needs anything."

I give in, but as we're loading a pale and sweaty Seb into the back seat of Reid's silver Porsche SUV, I wish Aggie had called an ambulance like I told her to.

It's exactly eleven minutes to the Aspen Valley Hospital. I can do this.

I hop in the back, pull Seb's head gently into my lap, and brush his dark hair out of his eyes. His eyes meet mine before fluttering shut.

"Hurry, Reid," I bark as we zoom down Dad's driveway.

"How long ago was he bitten?" My ex's bright blue eyes, fringed with golden lashes, meet mine in the rearview mirror. I loved his coloring back when we were together. When his wavy hair gets longer, it's shot through with streaks of honey and auburn. So different from the dark haired, olive skinned man whose head rests in my lap now.

"Ten minutes?" I shiver, remembering the moment the rattler struck.

"He must really love you to risk a snake bite for your cat," Reid says. He adds in a low voice, "Not that I wouldn't have done the same."

He glances at Seb, who seems to have passed out. His breathing is shallow.

"Have you thought more about what we talked about last night?"

"Not now, Reid."

I grit my teeth, determined not to say another word to him until we get to the hospital. I need Seb to get better, and then I can deal with my ex, my family, and the Everest-sized mess I've made.

Chapter Thirty

Beatrix

Reid pulls into the ambulance lane in front of the emergency department and, leaving the car running, jogs around to help me get Seb out of the car. Seb grits his teeth as if in pain, or like he might vomit. Or both.

Reid gently hoists Seb up and helps him inside, calling for help as we go. He was always very confident. Being so shy, I loved that quality about him when we were together. I'd always wished I were so self-assured.

I want to hold Seb's hand, tell him I'll be here for him, but I only have the chance to inform the male nurse who comes with a wheelchair that Seb was bitten by a rattlesnake before he's whisked away behind the imposing emergency department doors.

"I'll park. You check him in," Reid tells me.

I'm torn between wanting to thank my ex for getting Seb here quickly and wanting to smack him for giving me orders. He's not the boss of me anymore. Not that he ever was. Except that I sort of let him be. I shake my head. Having Reid here is messing with my mind. Now that we made it to the hospital, I wish he'd go home.

I check in with the receptionist, an older woman with a nametag that says *Carol G.* She motions me over to a blonde at another desk, *Sandy B.*

"You're with the snakebite?" Sandy B asks me as I sit.

"His name is Sebastian Ross," I say a little testily. "And yes, he was bitten by a rattlesnake maybe twenty-five minutes ago. Will they be able to give him anti-venom? Will he be okay?"

"Hon, I'm in registration. If I were a doctor, believe me, I wouldn't be sitting here." She snorts and chews a piece of gum that I swear wasn't in her mouth ten seconds ago. When she glances at my face, she softens, "Don't worry, we see plenty of snake bites. Haven't lost one yet." She thinks. "That I know of." She types something on her keyboard and studies the computer screen. "What's your relationship to the patient?"

Why did she have to start with the hardest question to answer? I glance around to make sure Reid's not behind me. "Friend."

She types that in, and I realize if Reid does come over, he might see it.

"Fiancé," I say. "He's actually my fiancé."

"Which is it, hon? Friend or lover?" She winks at me, still chomping the gum.

"Lover." My face flames. "I mean fiancé."

"Isn't that the same thing?" Sandy B looks flummoxed.

Not in our case.

"We're engaged," I say firmly.

"What's lover boy's date of birth?"

Date of birth. Date of birth. That's an easy one. I memorized that. But the stress of the last hour is catching up to me. I wrack my brain; I can't come up with the numbers. I'm doing the math with his age, trying to at least get his birth year right.

"October!" I say. "Nineteen ninety something."

She eyes me, one penciled eyebrow arching.

I can't remember the year. Sweat rises on my face and I yank on the collar of my t-shirt to release the bloom of heat growing under there.

"October . . ." I close my eyes, and the date comes to me. "October seventeenth! Um, nineteen ninety—"

"October seventeenth, nineteen ninety-two," Reid says smoothly from behind me. I whirl around. He's reading off a driver license. "He's also five foot ten inches, he lives in Boulder," he reads the street address to Sandy B, "and he's an organ donor. What a selfless guy."

I snatch the license from him. Seb's picture is good. Every driver's license photo I've ever had made me look like a small, sweaty serial killer.

Reid hands me Seb's wallet. "It fell out in the back seat." He shoots me a sharp glance. Ugh, he totally heard me struggling to remember Seb's birthday.

"Thank you." My voice is cool.

Sandy B watches us with interest. "Does your . . . fiancé . . . have any allergies? That you know of?"

I eye Reid. "This is private information."

With a smirk, he strolls back to the mostly empty waiting area and finds a seat. I sit in front of Sandy B again.

"Not that I know of," I say quietly.

She pulls a face. "Then why'd you say it was private?"

"A lack of allergies is just as private as what allergies he does have." Does this woman not know anything about healthcare privacy laws? "What else do you need to know?"

"Does he have medical insurance?"

I dig through his wallet and find a card. "Yes!"

Sandy B shakes her head and covers my hand with hers. "You sure you two know each other well enough to get married? Trust me, hon; you don't want to marry someone you don't know well. When I married my ex, Sheldon, I thought I was his princess and he was my knight in shining armor. Well, a year later, he realized he liked being the princess and went to find his own knight. I'm telling you, be sure you know 'em first."

I sigh. "Thank you for the advice. Do you need anything else?"

"Not for now."

"Can I go back and see Seb?" I ask.

"They'll come out for you. Go have a seat with your other friend. I don't know about your fiancé, but *that* one is all man." She eyes Reid, who's looking at his phone. He does manage to look dashing even in a lumpy hospital chair at nine in the morning.

"Yes, well, you haven't seen my fiancé. He's dark and handsome. Look." I hand her Seb's driver's license. She glances from it to Reid.

"You've got good options, hon. But make sure you really know them both before you pick one."

"No, it's not like that," I say. "I . . . oh, never mind."

I collapse in the seat next to Reid, and he puts an arm behind my chair.

"He'll be fine, Bea."

I smooth my hair back. My ponytail feels like it's been sucked through a blender. "I'm just worried."

"You must be to not remember your fiancé's birthday." Reid smiles. But he always smiles. When he told me he loved me, he smiled. When he told me he wanted to break up, he smiled.

I don't answer. I want to tell him to piss off. Seb loves me and we're very happy, thank you very much. Only, it's not true of course. Seb doesn't love me; I don't even know if he likes me. But he faced a snake to save my cat. Not because he loves Fluff as much as I do, although he's sweet to her. He did it because he's an amazing person.

Yes, he took my money to come to Aspen. But he never once complained about my family, although they gave him plenty of reason to. He never made fun of my awkwardness or my dozens of cats. And instead of telling him again how much I appreciated all of that last night, I kissed Reid.

I run back to Sandy B. "I need to see my fiancé. Please, it's urgent."

"Hold your horses, hon. I'll ask." She picks up the phone and speaks with someone, telling them my name. She nods, gives me a sorrowful look, and hangs up. "I'm sorry, he doesn't want any visitors."

Doesn't want visitors? He doesn't want to see *me*.

"Please, I need to tell him something," I say. "This is life or death important."

Sandy B raises a skeptical eyebrow. "Hon, this is an emergency department."

Okay, life or death might have a slightly different meaning around here. I wipe my sweaty palms on my hiking pants. "Maybe not that important but right below it!"

"Trust me, whatever it is you have to tell lover boy, it might be best to do it when he's *not* on a cocktail of venom and painkillers."

She's probably right. And I'm not sure what I can say to Seb that will make a difference if he doesn't even want to see me. I thank Sandy B and walk back to Reid.

"Take me home, please."

Chapter Thirty-One

Sebastian

Yesterday was a day of firsts.

I rescued a cat. I was bitten by a snake and landed in the hospital. And I made a tough decision, one of the hardest I've ever made. I'm still not sure my answer to Frank was the right one.

After I saw Bea kiss Reid two nights ago, I'd crashed in an empty guest room instead of going to her room. Between the kiss, and Frank's offer, I didn't want to confuse things even more for her—or for myself. I'd tossed and turned all night thinking about what to do, but it was the kiss that made up my mind. I'd planned to talk to Frank that morning and then catch a Lyft back to Boulder, but thanks to Fluff versus the rattlesnake, I didn't get a chance.

Now, I'm sitting on my bed at Aspen Valley Hospital. My left arm is in a sling, puffy and discolored under the wrapping, but blissfully pain free thanks to the sweet, sweet meds. I'm ready to be discharged; I'm just waiting on my dad to pick up my bags from Bea's house and come to get me.

He'll bring me back to Durango to recuperate for a week or so before I head home to Boulder. I won't be slinging cocktails or shooting with this arm for at least that long, so this is a good chance to spend time with my parents. Evan isn't happy about me taking an extra week off, but he loosened up when I sent him a few pictures of the gnarly wound.

I'm expecting Dad, so I get a painful jolt when Bea drags my suitcase through the wide door, my backpack and camera bag slung over her petite body. Her face is extra pale and her eyes are red-rimmed, like she's been crying.

"Hey." My foot, stretched out in front of me on the bed, twitches, and I can't meet her eyes. "Thanks for bringing those over."

She puts the bags down and examines me, her eyes landing on the sling. "How are you feeling?"

I choke out a laugh. "Like I wrestled a rattlesnake and it won."

Bea winces, and her eyes fill with tears. "Seb, I'm so, so sorry this happened. What you did for Fluff and me . . ."

I offer her my hospital-issued tissue box. "You don't have anything to apologize for. I'm happy Fluff's okay."

She nods. "Which wouldn't have been true without you."

I wave a hand to dismiss it. "How's Aggie?"

She perches on the edge of the chair beside my bed. "Wretched. She won't come out of her room, and I can't get her to talk to me. She hasn't eaten. She's spent a little time with the twins, but that's it. I wish I knew what to do for her."

"Give her time. Your sister seems like she has a lot of pride. It might take her a while to process this."

"I'm staying a few more days to watch Kate and Will for her."

"And maybe spend some time with Reid?" I wallpaper a smile on my face, but the truth is that saying the guy's name makes me want to toss up breakfast.

She bites her lower lip and studies my expression, which I'm working hard to keep neutral and friendly.

"Maybe." Bea drums her fingers. "I have some news."

My heart rate picks up. She's getting back together with Reid. And I basically pushed her at him.

"Dad agreed to transfer the funds to me now."

My muscles relax. "That's great. Have you let CCR know?"

"Not yet. I want to have the money in hand before I get Vilma too excited."

"Good idea." I smooth the blanket beside me, but the wrinkles won't lie down. "So our evil plan worked, huh? Success."

"All thanks to you. You were tremendous."

I wince inside. I don't *feel* tremendous about what I'm doing. In fact, I feel sick—but that might be the strong alcohol smell in the room combined with all the drugs partying in my system. Anyway, she doesn't seem to notice.

"So, now that our contract is officially fulfilled," she licks her lips, "I'm wondering if you might want to have coffee or go for a hike sometime. I could meet you in town, or there are some great walks around my house."

I look at the door, wishing a nurse would come in about now and put me out of my misery. I can't meet Bea's eyes when I say the next words.

"Thanks, but I'll have to pull a lot of extra shifts at the Bitter to make up for missing work. I'm not sure I'll have time."

She goes very still for a second and drops her gaze to her hands again. I see the glassiness in her eyes, but I have to stay strong. I'm sure this is what she would want me to do, if she knew about her father's offer. If I go away, she has her money, and she has another shot with Reid if she wants it. And I had to admit she looked like she did the other night when she kissed him.

I'm doing the right thing by us both. Aren't I?

She comes over to the bed and holds out her hand. Her

expression is cool, and I hate it. "Thank you for a job well done, Seb."

I breathe in her citrus scent. I'd face ten more rattlesnakes to pull her into this bed and kiss her properly. Screw Reid, her dad, and the money.

But she'd have to give up too much for me. This was the way our relationship was always supposed to end.

"You're welcome," I say.

Our hands look good together—her small, pale fingers cradled in my tanned palm. But like when I'm shooting and witness something amazing through the lens—a coyote chasing down its prey or a hummingbird hovering above a wildflower in perfect light—I have to accept that the moment is beautiful but temporary. And I have to let it go.

Chapter Thirty-Two

Beatrix

A few days after Seb left, I sit on Dad's patio with Fluff and the pile of Aggie's photo books. Between scratching my cat's ears and flipping through the pages, I watch the twins play soccer in the backyard. Will insists on being the shooter, which means he can pound his goalkeeping sister with the ball at every opportunity. I have to intervene twice before Kate decides she's had enough.

"Aunt Bea," Will complains loudly, "Kate kicked the ball into the woods."

He stands at the edge of the trees while Kate pouts. Neither is brave enough to go after the ball after seeing Seb's snake bitten arm the other day, and I certainly won't let them. I'd rather buy them ten new balls.

I manage to get them involved in a new game, a mash up of tag and red light, green light, when the patio door opens and Aggie emerges.

I'd expect her to be pale and disheveled after several days

locked in her room on a self-enforced ration of water and crackers, but instead her hair is washed and styled, she's wearing makeup, and her blouse looks ironed. How does she do it? And how did the same uterus produce us?

I glance down at myself. I'm wearing sweats and my t-shirt that says *Sorry, I can't. I have plans with my cat.* It's covered in Fluff fur. I think I last showered two days ago; I haven't felt like doing much since I said goodbye to Seb.

Aggie sits beside me and watches the twins, who haven't noticed their mom yet.

"Thank you for taking care of them the last few days while I've been . . . ill."

Ill? She might as well have said *indisposed.* "You're welcome." I pause. "How are you feeling?"

Her clasped hands tighten, but her expression is composed. "I'm better, thank you."

I pull Fluff against my chest, screwing up my courage. "Aggie, I'm here. Talk to me. You *can't* be okay after everything that happened. Tell me how you're feeling."

"I don't want to."

My sister keeps her eyes on her children as she answers. Her voice is as calm as her face, but a single tear drips into her lap. She wipes her cheek.

"Beatrix, I have to deal with things in my own way, and in my own time." She takes my hand. "But I'm glad you're here."

And just like that, my anger and frustration with her fades.

"Ag, your gift is wonderful." I'd been looking through the books for the last hour, retrieved from the chair where Dad tossed them. "You did a fantastic job."

She swallows. "If only Dad thought so."

"He's an idiot. And so is Ben."

She blinks, and one more tear falls in her lap. But she squeezes my hand.

I wish Aggie would talk to me about how she's feeling and what she plans to do. I wish I could tell her what happened with

Seb—the truth this time—and ask her what to do about Reid. I wish my relationship with my sister were different.

But I can tell that she's offering me as much of herself as she can in this moment. And I decide to be grateful for that.

§

"Beatrix, come here, I want to talk to you," Dad calls to me from his study as I pass by a few hours later.

I've barely seen him since his party. I'd been right about his hangover. He went to bed after all the excitement with Seb and the snake, and he didn't come out of his room until dinner, but he seems okay now.

He gestures to the chair in front of his desk. I sit and will myself to relax. When I think about it, sitting in this chair has never led to anything good.

"What's up, Dad?"

"How is your sister doing?"

I sigh. "Who knows?"

"She won't talk to you?"

I shake my head. "Not much." I pause. "Have you tried?"

He clears his throat and slides a pen across the desk. "If she won't talk to you, she isn't likely to talk to me."

I take a deep breath. "I think you're wrong. I think all Aggie has ever wanted is to talk to you."

Dad waves my words away. "Nonsense. We talk all the time about the foundation, our investments—"

"That's not what I mean. I mean *really* talk. She's always wanted to be close to you, but you never let her in."

His face turns alarmingly red as I speak, but I press on. It's time Dad hears this. I have to believe that people can learn and change, even at eighty.

"Henry and I had Mom, but Aggie and Thomas looked up to you. They wanted to be like you. You didn't seem to notice."

My father's mouth thins, and I think he's about to tell me

where I can put my criticism and touchy-feely crap. Instead, the color drains from his face, and he looks out the window for a long time. When he speaks, he sounds more fragile than I've ever heard him sound.

"I didn't spend as much time as I should have with you all. Not even with your mother."

"It's not too late," I say. "Aggie needs you, Dad. Especially now. Talk to her, or better yet, listen."

"I'll think about it." He straightens some papers in front of him. "Have you spoken to Sebastian since he left?"

A now familiar pang clutches my chest. "No. This week was stressful and . . . we're taking a break. We need more time."

Like, forever.

Dad's face makes a strange shift. "Well, perhaps you could take the opportunity to spend a little time with Reid then?"

He's probably right. It was time to speak to Reid, even if I have no idea what to say. I pull out my phone and text him, asking if he has time to meet me. He responds right away, and we agree to get coffee in an hour and a half.

"I need to shower and change," I say. "Talk to Aggie, Dad. Please. If I can talk to my ex, you can talk to your daughter."

His brief nod is enough to give me hope that he will.

Chapter Thirty-Three

Beatrix

I meet Reid at Hot Shot, a new coffee shop in town. I need to talk to him somewhere with no history. The memories of our relationship haunt our hometown like ghosts. I'm seeking the sunshine.

Reid sits at a table outside when I arrive. And, crap, he looks good. He's wearing a crisp white dress shirt with the sleeves rolled up, gray pants, and Ray-Bans. I remember what it felt like to press myself against his tall, lean frame, and more than that, the shelter and comfort I found in him at a time in my life when I really needed it.

Then I remember what it felt like for him to shake me off like cat fur and walk away.

He doesn't take his eyes off me as I walk toward his table, which makes me glad I took a little care in getting dressed. I have on jeans, a pale yellow tank top, a short gray cardigan, and my favorite red flats. I let my hair air dry, so it's flowing over my shoulders in loose waves. I feel good, confident, but it may not be enough for this conversation.

Reid stands and pulls out the chair for me. Something he never used to do. Something, though, that Seb does all the time.

He sets a mug in front of me. "I got you a flat white with almond milk and a little sugar. I hope that's okay."

That was my drink when we were together. It's not now, but it was thoughtful of him to try.

"How are things at home? I heard Seb got out of the hospital," Reid says.

"You did? How?"

"I ran into Henry yesterday."

I sigh. This town is too small for its own good. I'd been giving Henry and Rafi updates since the party. The one thing I haven't told them, or anyone, is the truth about Seb and me.

I hadn't heard from him since I left his hospital room. I'd texted him to see how he was feeling, but he didn't text back and I didn't want to intrude. He'd made it clear he was done with us. Done with me.

"He's recovering." I hope.

"I'm glad to hear it." Reid sits back, waiting. He was always patient, too.

I sip my coffee and gather my thoughts. "I owe you an answer to your question."

"Bea, I want to tell you again how much I wish I'd acted sooner. I wish I'd told you I wanted another chance with you earlier. I know you don't want to hurt Seb."

If only I could.

Reid reaches for my hand, and I let him hold it. "I wish I'd told you the truth about your father's request for us to break up back then. He made it pretty clear that if we stayed together, he'd not only make my life a lot harder, but yours, too."

"Wait . . . what?" I pull my hand away.

Reid blinks and stutters. "I thought you knew. I thought your father told you—"

"Dad made you break up with me?"

"Well, not in so many words, but he made it clear our futures would be brighter if I gave you space to mature and worked on my business."

Anger at my father burns bright again. I cannot believe he had an active role in Reid dumping me. Even if he did it because he thought it would be in my best interest, it was flat wrong. And the coward didn't have the guts to tell me himself.

"We weren't kids, Reid. What could my father do that would justify lying to me and breaking off our engagement?"

"He could take away your future. Your *freedom*. Bea, you've always had money. You don't know what it's like to scrape and save, especially while living in a town that tosses its wealth around like yesterday's trash. I didn't want you to have to live like that."

He's acting like he grew up in subsidized housing. Reid and Jane's parents live in a perfectly nice two story in one of the few relatively reasonable areas on the outskirts of Aspen. It's hardly a hovel, although I understand what he's getting at.

"I wanted you to have everything you deserved, Rabbit, including your share of your parents' estate. I couldn't take that from you."

I shake my head. "So you broke my heart to ensure my future?"

Reid nods, seeming pleased I'm trying to understand. "Yeah, I guess you could put it that way."

"And your plan was to—what? Hope my father changed his mind? Hope I'd stay single long enough for you to make your own money?"

"No, of course not. I had to let you go and pray we'd find our way back to each other again."

"You aren't religious," I say.

"This hurt me, too, Bea. I didn't want to end our engagement. But your dad didn't leave me much choice."

I eye him. "You didn't seem that broken up about it." Then or now.

He twists his coffee cup like a light bulb, studying it as if it might hold a hidden message. "I guess I could see the wisdom in Frank's request, even if I didn't like it." He looks up at me, his blue eyes piercing. "Anyway, things are different now, for both of us. I have a successful business. You have your writing career, which I'm so proud of, by the way. You did exactly what you set out to do after you decided you wanted to write. And . . . you have Seb."

"Who you don't believe I'm engaged to," I say.

"Look, a few things the guy said were fishy. I thought either you two aren't that close, or—"

"Or he couldn't be my fiancé. That he couldn't love me." And he was right.

"No, of course not. I wanted to protect you."

"By going behind my back and talking to my father?"

"I didn't think you would listen to me."

He wasn't wrong there, either. But seriously, what's the matter with my father and my ex? Both in their own ways tried to control and manipulate me. They treated me as if I didn't know what was best for me. Or if I made mistakes, I couldn't fix them. Like normal people do.

"Are you telling me you were waiting for me all this time?" I ask.

"I dated a few women." He traps my hand again. "But none of them were you. You were my first everything, Bea. I couldn't forget you."

I stare at our fingers together and find myself wishing the hand holding mine was darker, rougher, and less . . . freckled. I wish it were attached to a smaller frame with eyes a rich coffee color instead of boring blue. I choose my words carefully.

"Reid, I'm flattered. And I'm grateful to know the truth. But—"

"You need time to think. This was sudden and unexpected, and you have your relationship with Seb to consider."

Reid wrapped all my concerns into one nice little sentence that he obviously thinks will lead me to forget everything, throw caution to the wind, and jump back into a relationship with him.

"No."

"You don't need time?" His eyebrows shoot up hopefully.

"My answer is no." I soften my voice. "I appreciate you telling me how you feel, but I'm sorry, I don't want to get back together."

His face pinches. "You should think about it."

"I don't need time, and I don't need to think. I need . . . space."

If this week has taught me anything, it's that I've wasted enough time thinking about my relationship with Reid. I needed him when we were together; I'd felt lost after Mom died. But things have changed. I have a career, a home and a fur family that I love, charitable pursuits, and plenty of challenges to work on, like coping with my social anxiety and making more human connections. But spending time with Seb was a good start; he showed me I could do it.

More than anything right now, I need to trust my decisions and myself. Unlike Dad or Reid.

I stand. "Thank you for coming. It was good to see you."

And I mean it. He gave me a gift this week. From now on, I can see him at family gatherings without hiding, stammering, and feeling humiliated. Maybe we can even be friends.

No matter how angry or hurt I feel by my father and Reid's decisions, I can't get too self-righteous. Yes, they lied to me for their own reasons. I've been lying to my entire family for mine. What makes me any better?

My phone rings on the drive back home. *Travis.* I pick up in a hurry.

"Are you back in Boulder yet?" he asks.

"I'm driving home tomorrow. What is it? Is Ever worse?"

"I wish I could say I have good news, but I'm out of ideas. I think you should come collect her. Some old fashioned TLC might be our last, best bet."

My heart sinks. "I understand. Can you bring her to my house or should I meet you somewhere?"

"Hang on, let me check my schedule." There's a pause. "I'll be up north of Nederland at the Lazy Dog Ranch tomorrow. Any chance you could meet me there?"

"Sure, but a ranch? Do you see horses, too?" I ask.

"Nope, not my specialty. A trio of sweet dachshunds has bad cases of diarrhea. They're pooping everywhere. I'll send you the address." We arrange a time to meet.

I head home to pack, avoid my father, and consider everything that changed for me this week. I got a little closer to my sister but probably lost a brother-in-law. I was offered a second chance with Reid and decided I didn't want it. I would have what I set out to get—my inheritance—and through it the chance to help countless numbers of cats.

But I lost Seb, and I might lose poor Ever. Was the rest truly worth it?

Chapter Thirty-Four

Beatrix

The Lazy Dog Ranch is an hour out of my way, but I don't mind. The views from the Peak-to-Peak Highway are spectacular. Then again, my gloomy thoughts are like gray clouds blotting out the beauty of the mountains.

I'm rehashing the family drama with a headache to match the dull pain, deep in my chest, that seems to have made itself at home.

Thomas snuck home yesterday to test the waters after Jane's bombshell of a revelation. He told me Ben was sleeping at a friend's house. Not *that* friend, though. Thomas thinks it's over with the other woman, and that Ben wants another chance to make things work with Aggie. Time will tell if my sister will give him that chance.

The situation with Seb is reversed. He doesn't want to see me, and after everything that happened, I don't blame him. But I've thought about him every spare moment. His easy smile, his love of nature and his art, the way he was so diligent and thoughtful in his job as my fake fiancé. And he rescued Fluff. I'll never, ever forget that.

Reid and I were together for years and being with him feels wrong. Seb and I were never together and somehow being with him always felt right.

But it's too late. Admitting all of this to him feels silly. We didn't date; we weren't even friends. We were nothing. Except, it felt like something.

I set my depressing thoughts aside as I reach the turnoff for the ranch, where a long gravel road leads to a good-sized wood and glass building that looks like the main lodge. Spread out on the hilly terrain beyond is a series of different sized cabins situated on either side of a creek that meanders through the property. Guests walk from the cabins over sweet wooden bridges spanning the creek while the occasional housekeeping staff, wearing forest green polo shirts and khaki shorts, hurries between buildings carrying towels and cleaning supplies. A horse barn and paddock are visible in the distance.

I get out of the car and sit on a bench with Fluff to enjoy the fresh air and sunshine for a few minutes. I have no doubt I'm in the right spot; Travis's cheerful blue Love & Pets RV sits beside my car. He'd texted that he'd meet me here when he was finished with his patients.

I'm anxious to see Ever. I spoke to Vilma about her on the way here. She said I could bring her back to CCR and they would do what they could for her. But I know how few resources Vilma has. She relies on the people who foster to pay for the cats' treatments if they possibly can. So I'll take care of Ever for as long as I'm able.

I watch the staff and guests as I wait. My family visited a guest ranch in Montana once when I was nine and in the throes of a serious horse obsession. Mom suggested the idea and convinced the rest of the family that it would be fun. And it was. We went out on trail rides, slept in a cabin, ate with other families in the lodge, and listened to ghost stories and cowboy poetry while snarfing s'mores around the campfire at night.

To say I was deliriously happy to explore the surrounding mountain trails atop my assigned horse, Topper, was an understatement. I cried and hung on to the neck of the huge golden horse at the end of the week, and I begged for a horse of my own for a year after. Dad agreed to pay for riding lessons. He'd probably made the right decision, since my horse obsession cooled and turned to cats later. But I still savor the happy memories of that summer vacation.

After a few minutes, Travis, Amelia, and two women a few years older than me walk toward the RV from the direction of the stables. The women wear jeans, riding boots, and one wears a cowboy hat, with her wavy black hair pulled into a ponytail over one shoulder. The other has blonde hair that she's wearing in a messy bun. Close on their heels are three adorable dachshunds. They run flat out, ears flapping and bellies barely clearing the long grass. Fluff jumps to her feet, back curved and hackles rising. I stick her in her carrier and stand to greet the group.

Travis introduces me to the women, Isabel Costa and Adelaide Miller. "Isa and Addie are co-owners of Lazy Dog Ranch."

"I'm jealous," I tell them. "You couldn't have a more picturesque spot."

"Thank you. It's work, but we love it," Isa says.

"How long have you owned the ranch?" I ask.

"About a year," Addie says. "We've been friends for eons, neither of us had families yet, and we wanted to be set free from our cubicles in the city."

"So we pooled our savings and bought this place," Isa finishes.

I can't help noticing Isa's smile is short lived, and Addie has dark circles under her blue-green eyes, but the dogs distract me from studying the women any longer. The canines are doing their best to shove three long noses into Fluffernutter's carrier.

My cat is pressed into the back corner, but she can't resist swiping at the intruding snouts every few seconds.

Amelia points at the pups. "This is Zip, Zap, and Zoom. Aren't they cute?" The dogs hop on their tiny back legs and wag their tails.

"Adorable," I say. "But they don't look all that lazy."

Isa sighs. "Wishful naming."

"Of the ranch, not the dogs," Addie adds.

Travis pats the closest dog on the back. "That metronidazole should knock out the giardia. If not, give me a call."

"I will," she says.

Isa says, "We need to get back to the office. Thanks for coming all the way out here, Dr. Travis. So nice to meet you Amelia, Bea." Addie and Isa shake our hands and walk back toward the barn with the dogs yapping at their heels.

We head toward the RV.

"Nice people," Travis says. After a moment, he adds, "I hope the ranch makes it."

"Why do you say that?" Amelia asks.

"Isa mentioned they were having trouble finding a head wrangler willing to work for what they can pay, and they don't seem to have as many guests as they should at high season," he says.

Running a guest ranch, where you have to be outgoing and upbeat with guests for months on end, is my idea of a nightmare. No wonder the women look exhausted. But it will be a shame if Isa and Addie have to give this beautiful place up. The idea of having a grand adventure like that with a friend makes me jealous. I haven't had a bestie since my short-lived job as an assistant copywriter for a publishing company right out of college.

Amelia holds the RV door for Fluff and me. The windows are open, so it's nice and cool inside. I set Fluff's carrier on the floor, where she peeks out, meowing curiously.

"How is Ever today?" I ask.

"See for yourself." Travis opens one of the cages affixed to the wall, takes the kitten out, and carefully hands her to me.

I stroke her dull fur. She's thinner than before I left for Aspen, and she barely moves. She eyes me for a moment before her gaze droops. I cradle her against my chest. Fluff watches us, her tail twitching.

"What's the matter, Ever?" I ask. "What's wrong, sweet kitty?"

"I've done every test and treatment I can think of," Travis says. "IV fluids perk her up, but then she fades again. She just isn't bouncing back." He pauses. "I'm not sure she *wants* to get better. Animals have a strong survival instinct, but we all need something," he glances at Amelia, "or someone, to live *for*."

I nuzzle Ever. "What can I do for her?"

"What you're doing right now. If we can't get her better, at least you can make her last days good ones."

I blink back tears, and Amelia looks away, her face pink and eyes glassy. I stroke the kitten, collecting myself, while Travis puts some instruments away and Amelia cleans the stainless steel examination table and countertops. I haven't had Ever long, but losing an animal is never easy.

When she finishes her work, Amelia leans against the counter. "I don't want to pry, but how did things go in Aspen? Did the plan work?"

I bury my face in Ever's fur for a second. I don't know how to answer her.

"Amelia, that's totally prying," Travis says.

"I don't mind," I say. "The fake fiancé idea was hers, after all." And I have no one else to talk to about Seb.

Amelia pulls the examination table back down from the wall and hops up, facing me with an eager expression. Travis shakes his head and laughs.

I tell them everything that happened as briefly as I can. Travis listens politely, but Amelia hangs on every word.

"Your poor sister," she says when I finish. "And I can't believe your dad! Actually, I could see my mother pulling a stunt like that. I still haven't introduced Travis to her—my sister Avery is enough family to start."

Travis squeezes her shoulder. "So where do things stand with Seb?"

I sigh. "Nowhere. He fulfilled the contract. Job's over." I don't tell them I asked to see him again. The rejection still stings. In fact, it's getting worse. I can't shake the feeling that there was more to Seb and me than a sheet of paper and a padded bank account, but with no other word from him, it's easy to believe I'm wrong.

"You have to talk to him again," Amelia says.

"Maybe she's happy to let things end the way they did with Seb," Travis says.

She scans my face. "Of course she's not happy with that. Look at her when she talks about him. She glows."

I squirm. "I do?"

"Definitely." Amelia nods. "I know a glow when I see one."

I glance at Fluff, who wouldn't be here without Seb. "I . . . miss him."

Amelia kicks her legs with excitement. "Then tell him that!"

"I don't think he feels the same."

"You won't know until you ask," Travis says. "Amelia and I almost lost each other last year because we assumed things that weren't true."

My heart thumps. I can ask him how he feels. Of course I can. I'm an adult. I can do anything I want.

"You should invite him to the Love & Pets Party," Travis says. "It's this weekend." He hands me a flyer from a pile on the counter.

Amelia smacks him lightly. "Pushy."

"I'm just saying. It's a good cause." He kisses her nose. "Seriously, I hope you'll come, Bea. And it would be great to meet Seb."

I tell them I'll be there. As for Seb, I don't know, but I can ask. I only hope I can live with his answer.

Chapter Thirty-Five

Sebastian

I've been in my favorite spot between a large spruce tree and a pile of rocks for twenty minutes when the sun finally sneaks over the ridge to the east. I got off work at the Bitter at my usual time last night, but I couldn't sleep, so I came up here to Left-Hand Canyon to shoot.

Crappy sleep, crappy attitude, crappy work. That's me since I left Aspen two weeks ago.

I slept a lot when I got to my parents' house. I thought it was the combined effect of the pain meds and my body healing from the snakebite, but even after a week, I was still in a funk. My parents were so worried that they made me see their doctor to be sure something else wasn't wrong.

The insomnia kicked in when I got back to Boulder. I fall asleep quickly, but I wake up a few hours later. I make meals and don't eat them. I come up here to shoot, but I don't edit the images. I hang out with friends, and I leave early.

"What's wrong with you, bro?" Javi asked yesterday after I almost snapped his head off for leaving a cabinet door open.

I sank onto the couch and rubbed the throbbing spot on my scalp where it had hit the door. "I don't know."

"Is it Beatrix? She paid you, right?"

I scowl. The payment had come into my Venmo account with no note. Just to make me feel even worse than I already did. "Yeah, she did."

"Then let's go out this weekend. It'll take your mind off your problems. After you pay the rent, that is. I covered you last month, remember?" Javi tosses a pillow at me, and I throw it back.

"Yeah, okay."

Only, I don't want to go out with Javi. I don't want to do anything except see Bea again. I realized it at four this morning when I woke up sweaty, my sheets twisted around me, and her name on my lips. I want to know what's happening with her family. How she left things with Reid. Hell, I want to be near her.

But I can't. I got what I wanted out of our deal and as far as I know, she did too. Her inheritance, her rescue facility, and maybe her *real* fiancé. I can't get in the way of all that.

A flutter and a low hoot in the spruce beside me draw my eye. It's still dim, but I can make out the silhouette of an owl. I bring my camera up to my eye. There's barely enough light to catch the image, until the owl turns to face the rising sun.

My breath catches. The bird has two different colored eyes. One brown, one amber. Heterochromia, it's called. Bea seemed embarrassed by it, like her eyes made her look strange. She thought people stared at her. I know why they stare: because she's beautiful.

I gently press the shutter, catching multiple shots of the owl. As I watch the bird, one thing becomes as clear as the hooked beak on its face.

Bea might not want me. Her family might not approve of me. And my bank account might slap me stupid.

But I can't keep Beatrix Fuller at a distance, only a memory to enjoy later, like my photographs. I need to see her again, one more time, and find out what's really between us now that the contract is paid in full.

Chapter Thirty-Six

Beatrix

I sit on the couch in a patch of sunlight, my laptop in my lap, Ever beside me. Felix is draped over my shoulders, Mushie and Misfit play at my feet, and from the sound of it, someone broke a plate in the kitchen. It's good to be home.

Fluff sits on the dining room table, pouting over the amount of attention I've poured on Ever and the rest of my cats since I got home. I'd cuddled everyone twice, cleaned the litter boxes until they shined, washed all the beds and bowls, replenished their food supplies, and otherwise ministered to their every need. The sheer amount of time I've taken is a sure sign I'm avoiding something. I pretend it's this book.

The Long Trail to Love has to be the most appropriately titled book I've ever written.

I've never had such trouble finishing a story. Usually they write themselves. By the end of a book, the plot lines and events should all lead to a neat and tidy conclusion. No surprises. But the characters are being stubborn. They know what they want to say, but they can't find the words.

Gravel from the driveway crunches outside. I glance at the time. It's Mike the mailman.

Mike lives up the canyon. He has short hair on top of his head and a long gray ponytail that looks like a stowaway from the sixties. I bake vegan treats for him at Christmas, which he loves.

Over the last few years of chatting when he drops the mail, I'd figured out he's a loner, like me. If I'm being honest, Mike *is* me in about thirty-five years. It's a depressing thought.

I don't have the energy to make small talk with him today. I want to finish this stubborn book, I want Ever to be better . . . and I want to see Seb. I wish he was outside instead, but that was as likely as Mike turning out to be my real, long-lost father.

"Bea, I'm your vegan mailman father," I say in Darth Vader's voice, scaring the cats.

When I hear Mike's truck recede down my driveway again, I bring the random assortment of flyers, catalogues, and junk ads in to my kitchen table, shooing Luna and Bandit off. Turn my back, and they'll shred it all for fun.

I sort through the pile. Most of it ends up in the recycling; my bills are all on auto-pay. So I almost miss the white envelope with my name and address handwritten on the front. I'd know that cursive anywhere.

I open it, fingers trembling. As if she senses I'm nervous, Fluff jumps on the table and sits, her emerald eyes on me.

The letter from my father is only a page long, but by the end I can barely breathe.

Dear Beatrix,

Thank you for attending my birthday celebration. I hope your trip home was uneventful.

I have news to share with you.

As you know, I investigated Sebastian after Reid brought up several concerns about how well you knew each other. My distrust of your fiancé grew when I saw he'd had another relationship recently, but as you didn't seem surprised or upset, I assumed you two merely had a rough patch.

Still, I was suspicious of Sebastian's motivations, as I've been with every partner you and your brothers and sister have had. So I created a small test. I offered him a generous incentive to break things off with you.

I stop reading, fury blinding me for a second. My ridiculous, meddling father and his ridiculous, meddling manipulations. This had to be what he was talking to Seb about the night of the party, and maybe why Seb never came back to my room that night. Why he was so standoffish the next morning. Why he disappeared from my life. Why didn't I expect this after what Reid told me?

But more than any of that I want to know what happened. Did Seb accept the money? My eyes jump along the page.

You'll want to know how he responded, of course. I've included his answer. Beatrix, whatever you decide to do with this information, know that I've always and only wanted the best for you, Aggie, Thomas, and Henry. I make mistakes, but I do love you all. What I've included in the envelope won't prove my love, but it should prove I trust your judgment.

I've said you need to be settled before I would give you your inheritance. I wanted proof you could make good choices for yourself. With your choice of Sebastian, I know now that you can.

With love,

Dad

A check is inside the envelope, along with a folded note. My eyes widen at the amount printed on the check. It's not the full amount, but it's enough to give Vilma the okay.

I unfold the note. It's dated the day Seb ended up in the hospital.

Frank,

You asked for a number, an amount. I can't give you one. Bea's worth more than money. A lot more.

I know you have your doubts about me. And I understand. I'm not sure I'm the person who will make your daughter happy. But I trust she'll make the right choice for herself. So I will thank you for your hospitality over the last week, and I'll step away to allow Bea to decide what she wants.

I hope you'll do the same.

Respectfully,

Sebastian Ross

I drop the note and run to find my phone. Please don't let it be too late.

Chapter Thirty-Seven

Sebastian

The Love & Pets Party is in a park on the west side of Denver.

Purring, Betty sashays to a stop in the parking spot. My mechanic was more than happy to do additional repairs once I had the funds. I get out and join the throng of people and animals wandering through the park.

A pavilion in the center shades a DJ, who's playing hip-hop at the moment. Vendors selling stuff like organic pet food, leashes, and bowls stand under various tents. *See the world with your pet!* A sign for a pet-friendly travel agent says. I wonder how many hotels are cat-friendly . . . something I never would have considered before I met Bea.

I got a cryptic text from her asking to meet me here at this time. She didn't say why, only gave me the name of the event and the address, but she did ask me to bring my camera. She better not want engagement photos of her and Reid. If she does, I swear I'll grab the nearest cat food bag and chuck it at him. I'm not a violent guy, but even I have my limits.

When I spot a bright blue-green RV parked nearby, the event name clicks. Bea said Love & Pets is the name of her vets' business.

I walk toward the RV, unsure where else to go. And then I see her standing in the sun, a hand shading her eyes. Bea. My breathing and my pace speed up. But I don't know what to say when I get to her.

"You came," she says. The guarded look she gives me makes me question all my decisions since that conversation with her father. I wonder what she sees in my eyes.

"I'm here." I raise my hands and then shove them in my pockets.

She gestures to a food truck, The Soul Bowl. "Can I buy you a drink?"

Sure, let's drag out the awkward even more. I stiffen my spine and get ready to hear whatever she asked me here to tell me. Then she steps near, I catch the familiar scent of her skin, and I'm hers all over again. I don't know how long I can stand not knowing what she's thinking.

We get our drinks and walk to a shady bench to sit. People, their dogs, a few cats, and even a turtle lounge on picnic blankets in the grass.

Bea can't seem to sit still. She sips her lemonade every few seconds and keeps adjusting the hem of her shirt. This one is white with small blue outlines of cats all over. This girl and her cat shirts.

I rake a hand through my hair. "What's going on, Bea? Why did you ask me here?" My voice sounds harsh, but I can't help it. The silence is agonizing.

She bites her lip. "I . . . was hoping you could take some pictures."

Pictures? I knew it. My hopes slip to the ground and smash all over. "Of who?"

"Of the party—the people and pets and things. Travis, my vet, could use some good shots for social media. This is the second year of the Love & Pets Party, and he wants to keep building buzz for next year. It's a great event; he's gives free and low-cost exams and vaccinations for pets whose owners can't afford to bring their animals to the vet regularly."

The disappointment that she only asked me here to take pictures is jabbing me somewhere around my throat. I pull out my phone. "I can take some shots, but this is all I have."

She looks perplexed. "You didn't bring your camera?"

"Couldn't."

"Why not?"

"I sold it."

"But why?"

"To give you this." I pull a stuffed envelope out of my back pocket and hand it to her.

She opens it and stares at the huge wad of cash inside. "Seb, I don't want your money."

"That's good, because I don't want your money either. Or your family's." I gesture to the envelope. "That should cover some of what you paid me. I'll get you the rest as soon as I can."

She closes the envelope. When she speaks, her voice is a shaky whisper. "I didn't ask you here to take pictures."

I lean in and force her to meet my eyes. "Then why did you, Bea?"

Chapter Thirty-Eight

Beatrix

My body tenses, ready to run far away from Seb, from my family, from anyone who can hurt me. My fur babies might scratch, but the wounds are only skin-deep.

Except, I've run before. After Mom died and Reid broke up with me, I retreated into my work, my home, my cats. And although I'm safe, I'm lonely. I miss my siblings, difficult as they might be. I miss having friends to spend time with. And I miss being with Seb.

I look at his handsome face, tousled dark hair, and kind eyes. How did he become so important to me in such a short time?

"I want to apologize," I say. "My father told me about his offer. I'm sorry he thought he could buy you off. I guess I did the same thing. Like father, like daughter." I smile thinly. "Only, everything has changed for me."

Seb looks away, his expression hard. "Reid."

"What?"

"You said everything changed. You're back with Reid."

I pull my leg up on the bench so I can face him. "Seb, no. There's nothing between Reid and me anymore."

He stares hard at my face, as if his eyes could drill the truth out of me. "Are you serious?"

"Yes. And I told him so." I swallow, feeling lightheaded, but I press on. "I asked you here because I want a chance to have a real friendship with you. No more faking, no more lies. I want to see where this," I point back and forth between us, "might go."

He shakes his head. "It's too late."

I'd written plenty of scenes where my characters were rejected over the years. Their hearts sink, their stomachs clench, their limbs go numb, they freeze. They cry or run. I did all those things after Reid.

Not this time. I'm not giving up on Seb without a fight. As strange as our relationship has been, we have a connection worth fighting for.

I lift my chin. "Why?"

He lets out a long breath and then squints at me with a slow smile. "I can't be friends with you . . . because I've already fallen for you."

My hand flies to my mouth. *Is this happening?*

"That's the other reason I sold my camera. The deal was that if I fell in love, I had to sell my most prized possession, right? So I did." He takes my hands. "Anyway, my Canon wasn't the best thing in my life anymore. You are, Bea."

My eyes swim. "Are *you* serious?"

"Deadly. When your father bribed me to go away, I realized that money could always be between us. The money you paid me, your dad's money, your inheritance. So I said no thanks to him, and I sold my camera to pay you back. I thought maybe we could have a fresh start."

"I want that, too, Seb. But your camera—"

"I'll pick up extra shifts. In a few months, if I stay focused, I can get the 5D I've wanted forever. Although to be fair, you should probably give Fluff away so we're even."

When I eye him, he grins. "You know I don't mean it. I almost lost an arm for that cat. She owes me some serious cuddling on your couch or mine. I'm not particular."

His eyes meet mine, and his hand slides through my hair, finding the back of my neck. I cup his face, savoring the feeling of his smooth skin. He pulls me to him, and for once, I allow myself to dissolve into the moment. As our mouths meet, soft and searching that gives way to determined and dogged, I can feel the potential between us. The trust and affection. If we can work our way out of a fake relationship to real love, we can conquer any problem together. I want that, and miraculously, he does, too.

After a few minutes that will definitely inspire a hot new kissing scene in my book, I pull Seb to his feet.

"Come meet Travis and Amelia! If it weren't for them, we would never have met."

As we stroll, our arms around each other, I marvel at how my life has changed since last year's Love & Pets Party when I came late and left early with a panic attack looming. Today, the sun is brighter, the sky bluer, and the grass full of kittens and puppies. Oh wait, that part's true.

And I realize it's not that my life has changed. *I've* changed. All because of a ridiculous contract—and him.

Epilogue

Beatrix

"It's almost six, Beatrix," Seb rhymes from the kitchen.

I focus on the computer screen and put the finishing touches on a chapter of my latest manuscript. Since Seb and I started dating six months ago, I'd not only completed the final scene of *The Long Trail to Love*—finally—but I'd published two more novels in the series and produced a boxed set. Let's just say that our relationship provided plenty of romantic material for my writing.

"All right you two, playtime's over. We have to get ready for our guests." Fluff and Ever are tousling on the floor next to my chair. Ever rarely leaves her older sister alone.

The kitten turned the corner within weeks of coming home with me. She's grown to an astonishing twelve pounds, her gray fur is thick and lustrous, and her green eyes glow with health. She has quite the mischievous personality, too. Like now—she's getting ready to pounce on Fluff again, so I pluck her up, despairing at the amount of cat hair I already have on the Christmassy red dress I put on earlier.

"Okay, what can I do?" I ask as I enter the kitchen, but my words dribble off when I'm struck, for the twentieth time this week, by how lucky I am.

Seb's leaning over the counter with an apron tied around his waist, arranging fruit on a plate with a homegrown mint garnish. His hair is in his eyes, and naughty Nicky perches on his shoulders. After her surprise attack the first time he visited my house, she decided he was hers, and she sits on him whenever possible.

He straightens, catches Nicky as she slides off, and kisses me. "Ready for this?"

"I—guess?" I'm nervous. My family's finally coming to my house for a Christmas party, and I really want it to go well.

"It will be fine." His lips find mine again, and I press myself against him. We haven't even come close to getting enough of each other. "Aggie's bringing the kids, right?"

"And Henry and Rafi are driving Dad down. Thomas and Jane are coming on their own."

Ben and Aggie are still working on things. They've gone to counseling, and they've spent time together as a family, but Aggie's been slow to accept Ben's attempts to make amends. In my opinion, she deserves to have all the time she needs to heal from his betrayal. But she shows signs of softening—thanks to Dad. She told me on the phone the other day they've talked more the last few months than they have in years.

I survey the appetizers. We have the fruit, two kinds of finger sandwiches—meat and vegan, crudités and dips, and plenty of non-alcoholic drinks. With my family's encouragement, Dad's reluctantly climbing onto the wagon, and we don't want to make it harder for him than it has to be.

We'd almost made a platter of oysters for Aggie, but I couldn't bear the thought of serving seafood as a joke. Seb and I are still figuring out a compromise for our varying diets—but I usually win.

"You still want some family pictures?" Seb asks.

"Yes! Dad grumbled, but whatever. He owes me."

Seb finally got his new camera, the coveted 5D, a month ago, and he's been shooting nonstop. I'd offered to buy it for him, but he wanted to earn it himself.

Seb and I had gone back to Aspen in the fall to explain everything to them, right down to the lie-infested details. It had been a hard conversation—much harder than saying goodbye to Reid the second time—but everyone took it well, considering.

"I was worried you were going to tell us you broke up," Henry had said. "Instead you had a fake engagement, broke up, and now you're back together." He'd wrinkled his nose. "Actually, I'm still confused."

"Did you hear from Vilma?" Seb asks.

"We're on schedule to break ground in March as planned." I bite a carrot with satisfaction. Vilma was so excited about the funding that she'd made vegan tamales for me every month since September. We're serving some tonight.

I help Seb arrange the platters in the fridge. If we set them out before everyone arrives, the cats will take that as an invitation to play toss-the-crudités.

There aren't as many fur babies in the house as there were six months ago. A few of the older cats passed away, including good old Jinx, and I'd promised myself and Seb that I wouldn't adopt any to replace them. Seb had gently persuaded me that I don't need to take in dozens of rescues to be a heroic cat mama. And soon we'd have the new no-kill adoption center. Maybe then I won't feel a personal responsibility to rescue them all. Maybe.

"Come on, let's have a glass of champagne before they get here." Seb pours two glasses, and we sit on the couch in front of the lit fireplace. I snuggle in beside him, followed by Ever and Fluff.

"Beatrix Fuller, I have something to give you," Seb says.

My grip tightens on the glass as I take a sip, but I try to stay calm. "You do?"

"Yes, but you have to promise to give it back."

Give it back?

He pulls a square, polished wood box from his pocket and opens it. My breath catches. Inside is the most gorgeous vintage diamond ring I've ever seen. He slides it on my finger, and I move my hand back and forth to catch the light.

"Do you like it?" he asks.

"I love it . . . but why do I have to give it back?"

"Do you think I'm going to be called not a gentleman again? If your dad says okay, you can keep the ring."

I close my fist. "I'm keeping it. Dad can deal."

We both look at the diamond, a promise of years to come, and Seb's face grows serious.

"Will you marry me, Bea? Because I love everything about you, from your cat fur," he plucks a stray tuft off my shoulder, "to the way you always make me feel important, no matter how many words you have to write or litter boxes you have to clean. You're all I want to see when I wake up, before I fall asleep, and every minute in-between."

We share a sweet, lingering kiss.

"Well, that's a relief," I say. "Because I love everything about you, too. I can't imagine my life without you, Seb. And I don't ever want to try."

I mean it with all my heart. Despite my sad efforts not to fall in love, my fake fiancé will be my real live husband, and I have a sneaking suspicion he'll be an outstanding one at that.

I couldn't have written a better ending if I'd tried.

THE END

It all started with a girl, a boy, and a pug named Doug.
Get the exclusive Love & Pets prequel for FREE!

Love & Pets Book 3: She hates him and he hates her dachshunds. It's a doggone showdown!
Get your copy of The Downside of Dachshunds on Amazon now!

Read Next

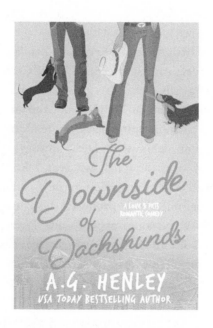

The Downside of Dachshunds: Love & Pets #3

Chapter One

Isabel

Dust swirls in a shaft of sunlight as I sweep the barn floor, trying to make the building presentable. I know how that sounds. It's a barn; it's supposed to be messy. But I can't help thinking that if the place is clean and orderly, maybe Tobias Coleman will take the job.

As I work, a few trail horses hang their heads over the stable walls, eyeing me while chewing mouthfuls of hay. When I finally clear the walkway, I look around with pride. The barn has never been this tidy before.

Stalls line either side of the walkway under the hayloft, and a good-sized tack room corrals the western saddles, helmets, and bridles used by guests of our dude ranch. Water buckets, barrels of feed, and piles of clean sawdust fill the area not taken up by horses, stables, and tack. The exterior of the two-story barn is painted a rich brown and bright white.

I pat my face with the candy-apple red bandanna tied around my neck. It's a warm August afternoon in the Colorado foothills. My phone camera tells me my mascara hasn't run and my thick black braid is mostly intact. My jeans are soil and sawdust free, and a swift glance at my pits allays my fear that sweat stains flood the folds of my denim shirt. Dust dims my ropers, but after Addie and I took over the ranch last year, I learned that clean boots were looked on with suspicion in these parts.

I glance at the time. Addie promised she'd be early so we can present a professional appearance. While I wait for her and Tobias, I stroke a few of the long, velvety faces that dangle over the stall doors. Apple nibbles a sugar cube from my palm and nickers in thanks. In the stall next to her, Parker's ears shoot forward.

I pause to listen. With a howl, the ranch's tomcat Rocky streaks across the barn floor and up Parker's stall door, making him rear. Following the cat, our trio of dachshunds Zip, Zap, and Zoom charge into the barn, trailing their leashes and barking uproariously. I jump back. They're covered in dark patches of what looks suspiciously like horse manure.

Rocky makes it to the hayloft where he hisses at the berserker dogs. They have no hope of catching him, but they're clearly determined to pretend they can. They jump up and down against Parker and Apple's stall doors on their stubby back legs. The horses shift back in their spaces, braying and banging against the walls.

Addie arrives last, panting and red-faced. My friend and co-owner is a wreck. Strands of her sweaty blonde hair stick to her face, one button of her matching denim shirt is undone leaving a gap where the bottom of her bra peeks out, and a dark smudge mars her cheek, which is alarming given what her dogs have apparently rolled in.

How did this farmer-in-the-dell-hell break loose in less than thirty seconds?

Jumping into action, I wave the broom to encourage Rocky to slink farther into the shadowy hayloft where the dogs can't see him. Then, I direct the bristles at the Zs to break their single-minded focus on the cat.

"Get the treat bucket!" I yell to Addie.

She runs to the tack room, and I hear her shake the plastic container. "Zs, treat time."

After a final satisfied glance at the loft, the dogs jog jauntily over to her, ears flapping. That's when I get a good whiff of them.

Ugh. I pinch my nose together with the edge of my bandana as Addie feeds them treats. We're totally rewarding bad behavior, but it gets them to focus.

"What happened?" I ask her.

My friend raises her hands, her expression bewildered. "I cut across the meadow from the cabins to make sure I got here on time. Rocky was asleep on a hay bale until the Zs caught wind of him. They pulled their leashes out of my hand and chased him, slipping and sliding in the poop—"

"Manure," I remind her. We're trying to use the right ranching words as much as possible.

She rolls her eyes. "Isa, if it looks like poop, smells like poop, and—" She makes a face, yanks a towel off the wall normally used for wiping down the saddles, and cleans her left hand, which I realize is covered in filth. "*Feels* like poop, it's poop. I'm just saying."

"What happened to you, though?" I ask.

"I chased after them," she gestures at the dogs, who pant happily now, "slipped, and my hand dove right into a huge poop nugget."

She examines her fingers, her face twisting with disgust. I carefully take the towel from her and wipe the smudge off her face.

"I'm sorry," she says. "I know we need to make a good impression."

I sigh. "At least he isn't here yet."

I spoke too soon. The Zs, lolling at our feet, suddenly rocket toward the barn door. A man stands in the entrance, arms up like he's being robbed, while the dogs race around his boots, barking. They won't bite, although they definitely give the impression that they might.

Addie and I try to call them off, but they've completely lost their heads. We chase them around like chickens. Addie grabs the leash of the smooth black and tan female, Zip, and I get the lead of the red male, Zoom. But Zap, the hairy chocolate and tan male, evades every effort to reach him. Desperate, I scoop up Zoom, Zap runs to his brother, and I snatch him up, too.

Breathing hard, I glance down. Manure—okay, fine, poop— covers the front of my shirt and tops of my thighs, and I smell like the ranch's septic tank took me for a spin and spat me out. Addie's even worse.

I wrestle my disgusted expression into a smile and turn to the newcomer.

"Tobias?" I ask with as much dignity as I can muster. "Welcome to Lazy Dog Ranch."

Get The Downside of Dachshunds: Love & Pets #3 now!

Acknowledgments

The Love & Pets series is written for book lovers, pet lovers, and love-lovers, and I have many of the above to thank for their help with *The Trouble with Tabbies*.

Due to a tendency to itch, scratch, and sneeze when around cats, I don't have any myself, so early on in the process of drafting *Tabbies*, I asked my readers for help. So many of you shared wonderful stories about your beloved cats, which helped me get ideas for cat names, cat behaviors, and naughty cat antics. There are too many of you to name, but know that I read and appreciated all of your emails.

I also recruited a group of cat-loving readers who answered my cat questions and provided even more in-depth information. My wonderful Cat Consultants were: Sally Collingwood, Alex Smith, Dottie Lafferty, Molly Hamblin, Wanda Siesicki, Lisa Roth, Michelle Solimene, Rhojalia Leonard, Trisha Perry, Donna Jean Eno, Heather Bryant, Terri Guest, Saundra Wright, and Eleanor Foreman.

A Maine coon sized thank you to my beta readers, Lorie Humpherys, Heather Bryant, Sandy Grant, Kathy Azzolina, Terri Guest, Saundra Wright, and Dottie Lafferty, who spent hours of their time targeting typos, wrangling sentences into grammatical submission, and sharing what they loved (or didn't) about the book. Many thanks to you all!

Finally and always, I'm so grateful to my family, near and far, whose love and support allow me to continue to do what I love best.

Also by A.G. Henley

The Love & Pets Series (Sweet Romantic Comedy)

Love, Pugs, and Other Problems: A Love & Pets Prequel Story

The Problem with Pugs

The Trouble with Tabbies

The Downside of Dachshunds

The Lessons of Labradors

The Predicament of Persians

The Conundrum of Collies

The Pandemonium of Pets: A Love & Pets Christmas

The Love & Pets Series Box Set: Books 1 - 3

The Brilliant Darkness Series (Young Adult Fantasy)

The Scourge

The Keeper: A Brilliant Darkness Story

The Defiance

The Gatherer: A Brilliant Darkness Story

The Fire Sisters

The Brilliant Darkness Boxed Set

Novellas (Young Adult Fantasy)

Untimely

Featured in *Tick Tock: Seven Tales of Time*

Basil and Jade

Featured in *Off Beat: Nine Spins on Song*

The Escape Room

Featured in *Dead Night: Four Fits of Fear*

About the Author

A.G. Henley is a *USA Today* bestselling author of contemporary and fantasy books and stories, including the Love & Pets sweet romantic comedy series. The first book in her young adult Brilliant Darkness series, *The Scourge*, was a Library Journal Self-e Selection and a Next Generation Indie Book Award finalist. She's also a clinical psychologist, but she promises not to analyze you . . . much.

Find her at:
aghenley.com
Email Aimee

Made in the USA
Monee, IL
24 February 2021